"Why this sudden urge to take me on a picnic?

"Why now, when for the past week you've been doing your best imitation of a poker-faced butler?" Bonnie asked.

"Because you looked like you needed cheering up?"

Judging from the skeptical lilt of Bonnie's eyebrow, Spencer guessed his glib response didn't satisfy her. He didn't want to burden her with the grisly details of his internal struggle, but he owed her an explanation that was a little closer to the truth.

"I've been trying to resist you," he said, scooting across the cloth until he was mere inches away from her. "But I've come to the conclusion that you're completely irresistible."

And she was. Seemingly without either of them moving, she was in his arms—almost as if she'd materialized there. Her lips met his with no trace of her previous shyness. He tried his best to maintain a gentle kiss, a *respectful* kiss, but there was no way he could.

Dear Reader:

1990 is in full swing, and so is Silhouette Romances' tenth anniversary celebration—the DIAMOND JUBILEE! To symbolize the timelessness of love, as well as the modern gift of the tenth anniversary, we're presenting readers with a DIAMOND JUBILEE Silhouette Romance title each month, penned by one of your favorite Romance authors.

This month, visit the American West with Rita Rainville's *Never on Sundae*, a delightful tale sure to put a smile on your lips. Losing weight is never so romantic as when Wade Mackenzie is around. He has lovely Heather Brandon literally pining away! Then, in April, Peggy Webb has written a special treat for readers—*Harvey's Missing*. Be sure not to miss this heartwarming romp about a man, a woman and a lovable dog named Harvey!

Victoria Glenn, Annette Broadrick, Dixie Browning, Lucy Gordon, Phyllis Halldorson—to name just a few—have written DIAMOND JUBILEE titles especially for you.

And that's not all! This month we have a very special surprise! Ten years ago, Diana Palmer published her very first romance. Now, some of them are available again in a three-book collection entitled Diana Palmer Duets. Each book will have two wonderful stories plus an introduction by the author. Don't miss them!

The DIAMOND JUBILEE Celebration, plus special goodies like Diana Palmer Duets, is Silhouette Books' way of saying thanks to you, our readers. We've been together for ten years now, and with the support you've given to us, you can look forward to many more years of heartwarming, poignant love stories.

I hope you'll enjoy this book and all of the stories to come. Come home to romance—Silhouette Romance—for always!

Sincerely,

Tara Hughes Gavin
Senior Editor

KAREN LEABO

Domestic Bliss

Silhouette **Romance**

Published by Silhouette Books New York

America's Publisher of Contemporary Romance

SILHOUETTE BOOKS
300 E. 42nd St., New York, N.Y. 10017

ISBN: 0-373-08707-1

First Silhouette Books printing March 1990

Printed in the U.S.A.

KAREN LEABO

credits her fourth-grade teacher with initially sparking her interest in creative writing. She was determined at an early age to have her work published. When she was in the eighth grade she wrote a children's book and convinced her school yearbook publisher to put it in print.

Karen was born and raised in Dallas but now lives in Kansas City, Missouri. She has worked as a magazine art director, a free-lance writer and a textbook editor, but now she keeps herself busy full-time writing about romance.

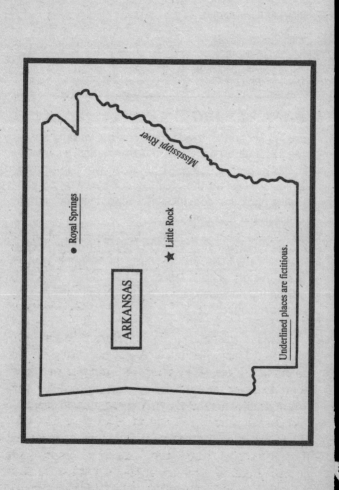

Prologue

Jenny, why don't you tell us what happened when you applied for a job with the local fire department." Professor Spencer Guthrie rolled up the sleeves of his blue button-down as he listened to his most outspoken student, a young woman with the size and temperament of an Amazon.

"I faced a classic example of sexism at its most blatant," said Jenny, twisting a lock of her carrot-red hair around her finger. "The admissions director was reluctant to hand me the application." She proceeded to outline, in detail, how she had been discriminated against.

"That was a terrific summary, Jenny," Spencer said. "I'll look forward to reading your full report at the end of the term. Now, who's next?" he asked, scanning the intimate group of eight bright graduate students. Sociology 407, the only course he was teaching this summer, was so small Spencer could afford to be informal. Today they were meeting at Mugs, a favorite student hangout just off campus.

"How about you, Randy? You've been awfully quiet today."

The class's only male student looked down at his lap and mumbled something unintelligible.

"I'm sorry?" Spencer leaned closer.

"I said I didn't do the assignment. I couldn't go through with it."

Spencer's brow wrinkled in concern. Randy Hoskins, whom the girls in the class had nicknamed their "token male," was one of Spencer's most enthusiastic students. He had seemed truly concerned about discrimination in the workplace, which was the thrust of this class. His sudden failure was unexpected.

"What's the problem, Randy?" Spencer prodded.

"I just couldn't do it, that's all." Randy clenched his fists on the table in front of him. "If I could type, maybe I could have applied somewhere as a secretary. But I found the only traditional female job I could do was domestic work, as a...a maid. And I'm sorry, Dr. Guthrie, but it's just like you've been teaching all semester. I'm a product of sexist programming." Randy looked around at the other students apologetically.

Predictably Jenny was the first to react. "Is there something *wrong* with housework, Randy?"

Celia Fredericks, another of Spencer's more vocal students, jumped in. "Anyway, *maid* is a sexist word."

Spencer leaned back, waiting expectantly for the next volley. An argument like this always made for a productive class.

"What's so awful about applying for a housekeeper's job?" Jenny challenged. "I'll bet Dr. Guthrie has worked at lots of traditional women's jobs in the course of his research, haven't you?" She turned and smiled sweetly at Spencer.

Spencer felt eight pairs of eyes on him and a decided shift of interest away from Randy. Suddenly his collar was unaccountably tight. "I'm the only male professor in my department," he began, but Randy cut him off.

"Being a professor has been a man's role until recently," he said. "That doesn't count. Have you ever worked as a secretary? Or a kindergarten teacher? Or a maid—I mean, housekeeper?"

The class waited breathlessly for Spencer's response. He could have lied easily enough. But the truth was, he hadn't ever taken on a traditional woman's role. He'd read about it, written about it, made speeches, conducted surveys and observed his students, but he'd never done it himself. He struggled to form the right response and failed.

"So," Jenny said smugly. "This is all just a bunch of talk, then. You're like all the rest of the closet chauvinists. You make pretty speeches about how we women have to fight for equality—so long as you have a secretary to type your papers and make your coffee."

"I make my own coffee," Spencer objected, knowing it was a feeble defense. A group of students who had, for eight weeks, hung on his every word had suddenly turned hostile.

"I don't think it's fair of you," said Randy, "to ask us to do what you haven't done yourself."

From the looks of the other students, they all agreed. Spencer ran one nervous hand through his thick sandy hair. Now what?

Randy held out a folded newspaper to Spencer as if in reply to the silent question. "The ad's right there, circled in red. That's the one I was going to apply for."

Spencer took the paper and scanned the Help Wanted ad, then read it aloud: "'Maid, cleaning and cooking duties for small resort hotel. Live-in position. Flexible hours. Apply in person, Sweetwater Inn.'" Then he looked again at his students, whose faces were masked with skepticism.

"You don't think I can do this, do you?" he said.

"Forgive me, Professor Guthrie, but I can't see you wearing an apron," Jenny said with a snicker.

Spencer narrowed his eyes, meeting the inquisition head-on, and stamped out his cigar. "I could go out tomorrow and get this job. And I wouldn't be embarrassed or uncomfortable in the least!"

Not one student appeared to be convinced.

"I'll do the assignment if you will," Randy counter-challenged.

"All right then." Spencer had to do something—he saw his credibility on the line, and he could never resist a challenge. "I'll not only apply for that job, I'll get it. And I'll work there the rest of the summer. And then I'll prove once and for all that I'm not asking my students to do anything I wouldn't do."

Later, as he bicycled up the long hill toward the sociology building, he started to wonder about something. He'd been teaching this graduate class for years, in California and now in Royal Springs, Arkansas. Why hadn't he ever done the employment assignment himself? Did he think it beneath him? Or was he afraid he wouldn't succeed?

He'd soon find out. Either way, maybe he was due for a small attitude adjustment.

Chapter One

Bonnie Chapman ushered her most recent applicant out the front door as fast as she could without being rude.

"Honestly, the nerve of some people!" she said with obvious exasperation as she tucked a wayward strand of her gold-streaked hair behind her ear.

Hobbling to the nearest chair, a Victorian rocker, Bonnie eased her slight frame into it with a defeated sigh. Her crutches clattered to the floor beside her as she struggled to prop her cast-encased leg on the footstool.

Once again she silently cursed the circumstances that had caused her accident and put her in this predicament. What advice would Sammy have offered, if he were here? Absently she rubbed the gold band on her right hand, as if the action might conjure Sammy up like a genie.

And then she laughed at herself. If Sammy were here, she wouldn't be in this predicament in the first place, because he would never have allowed her to climb that ladder to paint the trim around the roof. Consequently she wouldn't have fallen off.

Sammy. It had been almost five years since Sammy had drowned in a boating accident at Deer Lake, and yet a day didn't go by that Bonnie didn't miss him in some little way. Not that she was still grieving; she'd accepted her husband's death long ago. But in five years she'd never grown completely comfortable as the sole proprietor of the Sweetwater Inn. There were still times, like now, when she longed for Sammy's firm leadership—the way he always *knew* what had to be done and did it.

The sound of Theo's shuffling footsteps brought Bonnie out of her reverie.

"I take it the last girl didn't do, either," Theo said, "so I brought you a lemonade."

Bonnie took a frosty glass from the caretaker's gnarled hand with an appreciative smile. "Thanks, Theo. I really need this. And, yes, the last applicant was terrible. She wanted to work only ten hours a week, and she expected room and board for that. Doesn't anyone believe in the work ethic anymore?"

"Humph," replied Theo, perching uneasily on the love seat opposite Bonnie. His large body had always looked slightly out of place amongst the Sweetwater Inn's delicate antique furnishings. "I think most young folks today don't even know the meaning of 'work ethic,' much less believe in it. But Miss Bonnie, you've got to get someone in here soon—today! That party from Little Rock is expected this evening, and half the rooms aren't made up yet."

"I know, I know!" Bonnie said. "The inn is about to collapse just from the weight of the dust. But the women I've interviewed so far—why, I couldn't in good conscience hire any of them. I swear that first girl just made parole yesterday. And then there was the one with tattoos who chain-smoked during the interview."

"What about that rather large woman with the red hair?" Theo asked, stroking his stubbly chin thoughtfully. "She seemed pretty competent."

Bonnie scrunched up her heart-shaped face in distaste. "Are you kidding? She scared me to death. Within a week's time I'd be working for her instead of the other way around." She sighed hopelessly. "Well, I've got to hire someone, I suppose. All right. All *right*. If the next one who walks through the door, no matter how awful she is, can strip a bed and scramble an egg, I'll hire her."

"Good for you, Miss Bonnie!" Theo clapped his hands. "Now, can I do anything for you before I get back to fixing the roof?"

Bonnie shuddered as she pictured Theo climbing that tall ladder. At least the wind wasn't blowing now like it had been the day she'd lost her balance and fallen. "What you can do for me is be careful, Theo," she said. "Can you imagine what would happen to this place if both of us were laid up?"

"Don't you worry none, Miss Bonnie. I may be old but I'm spry." He took her empty glass and his own to the kitchen, leaving Bonnie to face the next applicant—if there was one—alone.

Frankly, Bonnie worried that there might not be another applicant. Her small ad placed in the *Royal Springs Gazette* had resulted in only seven inquiries over the past three days.

Maybe she should have invested in some more flamboyant form of advertising, she mused as she perched on the edge of her stool behind the ornately carved registration desk. Absently she stroked the huge orange Persian cat who habitually took his afternoon snooze on the desk's polished surface.

The Sweetwater Inn was an oasis of tranquility to its guests, perched on a heavily wooded hillside with magnificent views of the Ozark Mountains from every direction. But it was also a nice place to work, Bonnie mused. She should know, she'd lived and worked here a good part of her life. But now she realized that her small classified ad hadn't communicated any of the housekeeping job's pluses.

She located a pad and pencil and began drafting out a second ad to run next week, one that would have applicants standing in line! She became so engrossed in her creative task that she didn't hear the front door open and close, or the footsteps that approached the registration desk.

"Excuse me?"

Bonnie jumped, fumbling with the pencil and dropping it on the floor at her feet. "Oh, dear. You startled me!"

"Sorry." He smiled easily, Bonnie noticed, with a flash of even white teeth. It was the sort of smile that made her insides turn soft.

"That's all right," she replied, pushing the pad of paper aside and reaching for her registration book. She sucked in her breath as she scrutinized the tall stranger who stood as straight and sure as a pine tree in front of the desk. He was somewhere in his thirties, she guessed. Nice jaw. Thick wavy hair the color of polished birch. He was a strong tree with broad shoulders. The analogy made her smile.

"You don't look like a magazine salesman," she said, "so you must be a guest. Welcome to the Sweetwater Inn. How long will you be staying?"

"I'm not here for a room," he corrected her gently. "I'm applying for the job you advertised in the *Gazette*. I'm Spencer Guthrie." He held out his hand to her.

Bonnie hesitated only a moment before taking the hand and giving it a healthy shake. The hand was firm but smooth—no calluses. The hand of a professional man.

"I'm Bonnie Chapman. I'm—I'm sorry," she said, stumbling slightly over the words, "but what job are you referring to?"

"Was there more than one?" Spencer asked easily as he released her hand. "I'd like to apply for the house-keeping position."

"Oh," said Bonnie, not knowing quite what to make of this pleasant-looking, smooth-speaking stranger with eyes the color of topaz. She tried to reconcile the man with the job opening, and failed. She found herself laughing self-consciously. "You must be a little mixed up, Mr. Guthrie. The job I have open is for a *maid*."

"Yes, that's right."

"But I don't understand. You *want* to be a maid?"

"I prefer to call myself a housekeeper."

"Then you've done this kind of work before?"

"Yes," he replied, but a tiny worry line furrowed between his eyebrows. "My mother died when I was just a child, and I assumed total responsibility for a large household at a very early age," he continued. "I can cook, clean, wash dishes, do laundry, iron. I'm very capable."

"But do you *want* to do this type of work?" Bonnie persisted. The man had to be addle-brained. Why would a good-looking, able-bodied, seemingly intelligent man like this Spencer Guthrie choose to make a living doing domestic chores?

"This is just the type of work I'm looking for," he assured her. "I'm attending school, you see, and I need something close to the university. I'm sure I would enjoy working in a lovely old hotel like this one."

"But you're a . . . you're a . . ."

"A man?" Once again he flashed that enticing smile. "Is there anything about the job that a man couldn't do?" he asked, sounding not the least bit defensive.

"Well . . ." Bonnie racked her brain. There must be something. Then she remembered her promise to Theo, that she would hire the next applicant who came through the door. "Can you strip a bed and scramble an egg?" she asked impulsively.

The strange question didn't shake his confidence in the least. "Of course. I can also polish silver and cook a palatable roast. I'd really like the job."

"But you don't even know how much it pays," Bonnie objected, thoroughly amazed at this ludicrous conversation. She couldn't hire a man as a maid. "And you haven't seen your room," she added.

"My—room?"

"This is a live-in position. It says so in the ad." She paused, half hoping the man would make his excuses and go away. "It's no problem, really," she said when he didn't reply. "Live-in positions aren't for everyone. Thank you for stopping by, Mr. Guthrie."

"May I see the room?" he asked, once again oozing assurance. "Although I'm sure it will be adequate."

Bonnie shrugged with exaggerated casualness and opened a small drawer, plucking a set of keys from its interior. "Whatever you say. You'll have to forgive me, however, if I'm a little slow." Awkwardly, she slipped off her stool, then reached for her crutches.

"Oh, I didn't realize," said Spencer as he got his first glimpse of the cast that encased Bonnie Chapman's leg up to the knee. His gaze lingered a moment on the rest of her shapely leg, then both legs, slim and tanned and set off to perfection by a full-skirted white culotte. "If you'll give me the key and some directions," he said when he'd found his voice again, "I can take a look at the room myself. There's no need for you to bother."

Bonnie shot him a grateful look, then handed him the keys. "Go through the dining room, into the kitchen, and take a right. Look for a blue door with a porcelain knob. That's the maid's...er, I mean, the housekeeper's room. There's a small private bath attached."

"Very good. I'll be back in a minute."

Spencer strode through the dining room, his head spinning. Of all the things he'd expected to find at the Sweetwater Inn, Bonnie Chapman hadn't been one of them. The moment he'd laid eyes on her, her head bent over some task, blond curls cascading negligently over one shoulder, he'd felt a slow burning start from somewhere deep inside.

When she'd looked up at him with those huge gray-green eyes, his knees had nearly buckled. And her voice! Like warm molasses over ice cream.

As he made his way to the kitchen, Spencer noted the warm antique furniture, the faded rugs, the hutch filled with Blue Willow china, the groupings of tintypes framed and hanging on the wall. This was a beautiful hotel, he had to admit, in need of some sprucing up, but charming nonetheless. It wouldn't be an unpleasant place to work.

He should have read the ad more carefully, however. He hadn't counted on living here. Perhaps that part of the job was negotiable. But would it be so bad? He was within bicycling distance of the university. He would have a private room and bath. And certainly the job would afford him enough time off to pursue his various research projects or social activities. No, living here for six weeks wouldn't be a problem.

The kitchen was well-appointed and clean, but the floor needed a fresh coat of wax. He supposed that would be his job. The blue door was there, right where Bonnie had indicated. He opened it and burst out laughing.

The room was a study in feminine decor. The canopy bed was bedecked with ruffles and flounces the color of cotton candy. A dresser and matching chest of drawers were made of white enamel, with porcelain knobs sporting pink roses. The wallpaper also featured a rose motif. Spencer, trying to envision himself ensconced in this fantasy of spun sugar, laughed again.

But then he sobered. This opportunity was just too good to pass up. Never had he encountered an employment situation that was so deeply ingrained with femininity. Bonnie Chapman, who looked and talked like a Southern belle right up to her delectable earlobes, was likely to be overflowing with wonderfully inflexible attitudes about men's and women's roles. And with each new guest who checked in came another chance to gather a fresh reaction to the male housekeeper.

He *had* to take this job, for the sake of research if nothing else.

Spencer had spent his entire professional life as a sociologist studying women's roles in society. He had a reputation among his peers as a champion of equality and women's rights, and was well-known for his often unpopular opinion that women could perform ''men's work'' as well as their male counterparts, and vice versa.

Each semester he challenged his graduate students to apply for a job that was traditionally reserved for the opposite sex and then to carefully document the results. This summer term, however, the tables had turned for Spencer.

So, here he was. If he succeeded he'd have the makings of a great article for one of the professional journals. If he failed, he stood to lose the confidence of his students and face the ridicule of his colleagues, who of course would all know by the end of the day what he was up to. The sociology department grapevine was notoriously efficient.

Gently Spencer closed the door on the Rose Garden Room and made his way back to where Bonnie waited for him, grinning playfully.

"Not exactly the accommodations you had in mind, I'll bet," she said.

"It suits me fine," Spencer replied, struggling to maintain a straight face as he returned her keys.

"And you still want the job?" Bonnie asked incredulously.

"Yes, as long as I can attend my afternoon class two days a week. That's my only stipulation."

"Oh, that's no problem," Bonnie replied, though she thought this Mr. Guthrie looked a bit mature to be a student. "I think it's wonderful that you're trying to, um…" *Darn*. She'd almost said "trying to better yourself." How snobbish that would have sounded! "What is it you're studying?" she asked instead.

"Sociology. I'm interested in the research end." That wasn't a lie, he told himself.

"Are you close to graduating?"

He hesitated. "Not really. Is there any special clothing required for this job, Ms. Chapman, or is what I'm wearing all right?"

She swallowed the urge to correct his *Ms.* to *Mrs.* She'd always disliked the ambiguous title of *Ms.* But how important was a title, anyway? "Please call me Bonnie," she said instead. Surveying his clothing with a critical eye, she could find nothing amiss with his immaculate white button-down shirt and his neatly creased khaki slacks, which emphasized the muscular lines of his thighs without being snug. "Yes, what you're wearing is fine. Jeans are okay, too. We're pretty casual around here."

Spencer nodded. "So when do I start?"

"Well, I haven't hired you yet," Bonnie said primly, but then she found herself smiling. "Oh, who am I kidding? You're the only applicant I've had who's even remotely qualified." She pulled some papers from behind the desk and handed them to Spencer. "You can fill these out later. If you can start to work immediately, you've got the job." There, she'd done it.

"How immediately?"

"Now. I've got four rooms upstairs that need making up, two bathrooms to scrub down, groceries to buy and a dinner to prepare for a large party that's coming in from Little Rock tonight."

Spencer shrugged good-naturedly. "Nothing like jumping in with both feet. But I have just one question."

"Yes?"

"What happened to my predecessor?"

"Your predecess—" Bonnie wrinkled her brow in momentary confusion until the light dawned. "Oh, you mean the last maid? She fell off a ladder and broke her ankle."

Spencer nodded his understanding. "So you've been doing all the work yourself until now?"

"Yes, I'm afraid you're the first maid I've ever hired. You see, I've always done the housework around here, since I was just a kid. Long before I married Sammy. But I can tell you from ten-plus years of experience that it's not a bad—"

"Sammy? Oh, you have a...I mean—"

Spencer's less-than-graceful reaction to the news of Bonnie's marital status was interrupted when an old man appeared with a tray of glasses and a pitcher of lemonade. "Afternoon, sir," he said amiably to Spencer. "Thought you could use a refill, Miss Bonnie. Can I take this gentleman's bags up?" Then the man looked around, apparently perplexed when he saw no luggage.

Spencer inclined his head toward the man and looked at Bonnie. "Sammy?" he asked.

Laughter erupted from inside Bonnie at the thought of Theo as her husband. Why he was old enough to be her grandfather! Theo, too, she noticed, had cracked a smile but was trying not to laugh. Quickly Bonnie composed herself. "Spencer, I'd like you to meet Theo Johnson. He's been taking care of this place and everyone in it for—how long, Theo?"

"Fifty-two years come September," he supplied proudly.

"And, Theo," Bonnie continued, "this is our new—um—housekeeper, Spencer Guthrie."

Spencer held out his hand, but Theo only stared, his jaw hanging slack.

"Well, you *told* me to hire someone, so I did," said Bonnie defensively. "I think Mr. Guthrie will do a fine job."

Recovering, Theo took the hand that was proffered and shook it energetically. "Nice to meet you, young feller. If Miss Bonnie says you're all right, then I guess I oughta welcome you aboard."

"Thanks," said Spencer.

"And as for Mr. Chapman—Sammy, that is—he's been deceased for some time," Theo explained. "Care for some lemonade, Spencer?"

Spencer looked uneasily at Bonnie as Theo filled the three glasses on his tray. "I'm sorry—" he started to say.

"Don't worry, Mr. Guthrie, you haven't blundered. I'm not going to burst into tears. Sammy's been gone for five years."

"Oh. Well." Spencer cleared his throat. "I think I'll take a rain check on the lemonade, Theo. Right now I believe I have rooms to clean and groceries to buy."

Bonnie nodded, relieved beyond words that someone was actually going to get started on those impossible chores. "They're the four rooms on the east side of the second floor," she said. "Theo can show you the rest of the hotel later, if that's all right."

Spencer nodded that it was.

It felt strange to delegate duties, Bonnie realized. Theo was the only employee she'd ever had, and she never had to tell him what to do. He just did what needed to be done without asking.

She explained to Spencer in detail—probably too much detail, she thought later—where all the cleaning supplies were and exactly what chores needed to be done. And then she watched, with no small amount of appreciation, as Spencer bounded energetically up the stairs to start work. He had a cute tush.

"Sorry, Sammy, I couldn't help but notice," she whispered, her eyes directed up at the heavens. But deep down she knew Sammy wouldn't have minded. He'd been a dear, generous man when he was alive, and she was sure that no matter where he was now, he wouldn't begrudge her admiration of a wholly desirable man.

Upstairs, Spencer stripped the first bed of its sheets and pillowcases, stuffing the dirty linens down the laundry chute. That wasn't so difficult. Now where had Bonnie said the clean sheets were stored? Oh, well, he'd get to that later. Maybe he should tackle the bathrooms first.

Cleaning bathrooms had never been a favorite chore. Nor was he very good at it, he discovered a few minutes later. In his own home a lick and a promise was good enough to hold him until the twice-monthly cleaning service gave it a thorough going over. But when he viewed his own work with the critical eye of a hotel guest, he realized that a little elbow grease was in order.

Once he'd finished the first bathroom, he was pleased with the results, until he looked at his watch. He'd taken almost forty-five minutes! How would he ever get done in time to buy groceries and fix dinner for a crowd of people?

A small doubt began nibbling at his consciousness as he hastily stretched peach-colored sheets on one of the antique four-poster beds. He was qualified to do this, wasn't he? Sure, he'd laid it on a little thick when he boasted to Bonnie about his qualifications. But his mother really had died when he was young, and he'd taken on many extra responsibilities in the large household. He knew what to do with a scrub brush.

Still, knowing and doing were two different things. He had delegated much of the actual cooking and cleaning among his four younger sisters. Oh, he'd occasionally thrown together dinner or done a load of laundry, so housework wasn't totally alien to him. But was he up to Bonnie Chapman's standards?

He'd just have to work doubly hard to make sure he was. If he lost this job due to incompetence, it would just prove that his students were right. He would have shown himself to be nothing more than a windbag blowing hot air, and he wouldn't be able to hold his head up when it came to arguing about equality between the sexes.

Even worse was the prospect of Bonnie Chapman sending him away with his tail between his legs, never to see her again. No, that wouldn't do at all. He intended to use the full six weeks of summer he had left to untangle the mysteries surrounding that little lady.

Little lady? Since when had he allowed himself to use such a patronizing phrase, even in thought? Had Bonnie thrown him that far off balance?

She wasn't his type anyway, he decided, redoubling his housekeeping efforts. His taste in women leaned toward career-minded, sophisticated executives, liberated feminists who paid for their own dinners and expected to be treated as equals. Bonnie Chapman, on the other hand, probably couldn't open a door for herself even if she weren't on crutches. He'd encountered her type before; she oozed so much femininity a man could drown in it. In his experience, that kind of woman could be sweeter than maple syrup to your face, helpless and clinging, then ruthless and manipulative behind your back. No, thanks.

By the time he began on the fourth room, he was gaining speed. The bed was made in record time and the dust mop fairly flew across the floor. This wasn't so hard. He was almost done.

"Spencer!" The voice fairly floated up the stairs.

Spencer walked to the head of the stairs, thinking that even when Bonnie shouted, her voice was pleasing. "Yes?"

She gazed up at him from the registration desk, looking embarrassed. "Normally I wouldn't bellow like that, but bellowing is much easier than trying to get up those stairs to find you. I'm done with the grocery list. Are you ready to go shopping?"

"Just finishing up the last room," Spencer answered, adding to himself with a chuckle, *a man's work is never done*.

Chapter Two

So tell me about the Sweetwater Inn. It must have an interesting history.'' Spencer, sporting a starched white apron, stood at a large stainless steel sink in the kitchen, scrubbing the vegetables Theo had picked from the garden out back. Bonnie perched on a stool near a tall counter, shelling peas. A succulent roast browned in the oven; boiled potatoes sat on the stove, waiting to be mashed.

All in all dinner was progressing nicely, Spencer decided, though he knew he couldn't have done it without Bonnie's supervision. Cooking enough food for sixteen or twenty people was a formidable task.

"Ah, you've broached one of my favorite subjects," said Bonnie in answer to his question. "The history of the inn is part of what we charm our guests with. You'll need to learn it yourself so you can recount it, if you're asked. And if you work here for any length of time you'll surely be asked."

I'd better work here for at least six weeks, Spencer thought as he cut a small spot off an otherwise astoundingly robust tomato.

Bonnie began recounting her tale with obvious relish. "Colonel Joseph Chapman, a Southern gentleman from Alabama and a veteran of the Civil War, had suffered continual pain from an old war wound for more than ten years when he heard about the therapeutic properties of certain mineral waters that abounded in parts of Arkansas. So he packed up his wife, Miss Eliza, his two children Ezra and Lula, and headed for Eureka Springs, our town's more famous neighbor.

"Unfortunately, his wagon broke down, right about where you're standing—"

"A bit of poetic license, Bonnie?" Spencer put in.

"Well . . . we don't know exactly where it broke down, but it could have just as easily been here as over yonder."

Spencer smiled at Bonnie's deliberate exaggeration of her Southern accent. "Go on," he urged as he selected an appropriate tomato-slicing knife from a rack.

"Anyway, Colonel Joseph discovered that the mountains hereabouts were just chock-full of mineral springs. He claimed the spring water fixed his aching back up dandy, so he decided to stay and build a house. He also built a bathhouse and had the mineral water piped right into it. It's behind the main building—" Bonnie nodded in the general direction of the rear of the house "—and still works wonderfully."

"Then the guests come here for the baths?" Spencer asked. "Mineral water isn't really therapeutic, is it?"

"Shh!" Bonnie hissed. "If it isn't, we don't talk about it. And anyway, it may not cure everything the way our grandparents claimed, but our baths are as relaxing as any high-priced health spa whirlpool. You'll see."

"You don't mind, then, if I try them out?"

"Feel free whenever you like. I myself indulge on a daily basis—at least, I did until I broke my ankle; I can't get the cast wet."

Spencer cursed softly as he nicked himself with the sharp knife. He should have been thinking about his work instead of conjuring up images of Bonnie Chapman in the buff, *indulging* herself in a hot-spring bath.

"You okay?" she asked.

"Fine. Finish the story," he said, a little more gruffly than he intended.

Bonnie appeared not to notice. "So anyway, word got around about the wonderful mineral baths in Royal Springs, and pretty soon folks were dropping in from all over. The town boomed. The Colonel, being an enterprising man, opened his doors to visitors, and before long he had turned his home into a successful hotel. A painting of the Colonel and Miss Eliza hangs over the fireplace. I'm told it's quite valuable, although who knows?"

"You've never had it appraised?" Spencer asked out of idle curiosity.

"I was afraid to. I was afraid that if I learned its true worth, I might sell it," Bonnie admitted.

Spencer looked up sharply, then voiced what he knew was an impertinent question. "Why? Are you in financial difficulties?" He asked only out of concern, however. For some reason he hated to think of Bonnie struggling. It was difficult enough watching her lurch around on those crutches, frustrated because she couldn't accomplish some task or another.

But Spencer was relieved when Bonnie shook her head. "Not now. But it was touch and go there for a while."

"When was that?"

"You're getting ahead of my story," she replied.

"Very well. Please, continue."

"Let's see, where was I? Oh, yes. Both the Colonel and Miss Eliza lived into their nineties, and they claimed it was because of the mineral water. Their son, Ezra, fought in the Spanish-American War alongside Teddy Roosevelt, then came home and married a local girl. They had seven kids—all girls but the youngest, who was Sam's grandfather, Jesse. He inherited the inn—"

"And the girls got diddly, right?" Spencer couldn't help interjecting.

"The girls got healthy dowries, of course," Bonnie corrected, eyeing him curiously. "All but one got married and moved away. The sister who stayed behind, Aunt Sybil, we called her, died, oh, about fifteen years ago. I learned to cook by hanging around her in the Sweetwater Inn kitchen when I was a little girl."

"How did you know the Chapmans so well?" Spencer asked.

"This is kinda funny, actually," she said. "My mother used to be the maid here. When she died, I just sort of slid into her role. Let me tell you, the family was scandalized when Sam declared he wanted to marry me. I mean, he was the landed gentry and I was the penniless serf. But they got over it. Actually, there isn't any family around to object anymore. Sam's father died right after we were married, his mother retired in Florida, and his brother, Kenny—well, I don't know what's happened to Kenny. He—" Bonnie cut herself off, holding one hand to her head and sighing elaborately. "Will you listen to me? My tongue is wagging so fast it's likely to get a cramp. You shouldn't let me talk on like that."

"Why shouldn't I? I'm enjoying it." She could have recited the phone book and he would have enjoyed it. There was something about her voice....

"I'm supposed to be telling you the history of the inn, not my own life story."

"Tell me more about the inn, then."

"All right." Bonnie relaxed visibly as she continued the saga. "Grandpa Jesse passed the inn on to his son Calvin, who in turn passed it on to Sammy and Kenny."

"You started to tell me about Kenny a moment ago. What happened to him?"

Bonnie shrugged. "I'm not sure. Ken never was the responsible type, I'm afraid. Oh, he was lots of fun. In fact, when we were in high school I had a crush on Ken rather than Sam. He was considered a real hunk, as we said back then. I even thought I wanted to marry him. Sam, on the other hand...well, Sam was quiet, but he was sweet and fairly settled. Thank goodness I wised up and married the right brother." She gave a short self-conscious laugh at that.

Spencer studied her heart-shaped face and tried to read between the lines. She'd loved her husband, that much was certain. But was she still grieving for him? She smiled, unaware of Spencer's scrutiny. The smile seemed to be provoked by pleasant memories, for it wasn't a sad smile. She was over the tragedy of losing Sam, Spencer decided, although he didn't understand why that fact had significance.

"So Kenny moved on to greener pastures?" Spencer asked, hoping to get off the subject of Sam, which made him inexplicably uncomfortable.

"The last time I saw him was at Sam's funeral," Bonnie replied matter-of-factly, handing a strainer full of peas to Spencer for rinsing. "He took off for Europe—

Paris, I think—and I never heard from him again. I tried to find him once, even hired a private detective, but it seems he vanished. I can't help believing he's dead. After all, five years and not a word. That's too irresponsible even for Kenny."

"But he owns half this inn, right?" Spencer asked, wondering about the legal ramifications.

"That's right. To tell you the truth, I usually forget that anyone other than me owns this hunk of real estate. I run it as I please, and I don't worry too much about Kenny."

"You don't worry?" Spencer repeated incredulously. "Do you have any idea what sort of mess you'd have on your hands if you decided to sell this place? What if Kenny has heirs you don't know about?"

"In the first place, I wouldn't dream of selling the Sweetwater Inn." Her words had taken on a definite frost. "In the second place, I've looked into all the legalities, so you don't have to get all preachy on me." She paused, then took a deep breath. When she continued, her voice was once more calm and honey smooth. "When he's been missing a certain number of years, I can see about having him legally declared dead, but I'll worry about it when the time comes. How's that roast coming along?"

Spencer felt properly chastised. What business was it of his who owned the inn, anyway? Opening the oven door a crack, he sniffed at the escaping aroma. Wild onions collected from the surrounding woods and sweet bell pepper from the garden would give this roast a unique flavor, Spencer decided. "Another thirty minutes, I expect," he said. "What's next?"

"Do you know how to make dinner rolls?"

"Of course." *The frozen kind,* he added to himself.

"The recipe is . . . oh, I don't know where the recipe is. I've been doing it from memory so long I don't remember where I put it. I'll have to dictate it."

Somehow Spencer bluffed his way through the dinner rolls. Fortunately, Bonnie wasn't watching too closely. Her concentration was focused on a plate of radish rosettes she was carving, so she didn't notice when he dropped the eggshell into the batter, or when the industrial-strength mixer went a little out of control and sprayed flour all over the wall.

"Is there more to the inn's history?" Spencer asked when the rolls were somehow miraculously ready for the oven.

"This hotel has survived two tornadoes and a fire that took out part of the second floor," she said, reverting to her rehearsed monologue. "This kitchen, which used to be a screened-in porch, was added in 1924 and remodeled in 1965. And now you've heard everything that's for public consumption.

"The rest of the story is that—" she hesitated a fraction of a second, then continued "—is that Sammy drowned in Deer Lake one summer, and the business fell into my incompetent hands. All I'd ever done was cook and clean, so it was quite a shock to find myself a proprietress of the Sweetwater Inn. There were estate taxes and attorneys' fees to pay. Soon after I took over, we had a couple of bad years for tourism down here. But I had a little nest egg tucked away, and Theo floated me a small loan, and somehow we muddled through. The Sweetwater Inn is back on track, now."

Not a trace of bitterness, Spencer noted. Sounded as if she'd been through hell, and yet she talked about it all as if such rotten luck were a matter of course. Bonnie Chapman was tougher than she looked, he decided.

Maybe she wasn't quite the cream puff she'd originally appeared to be.

Bonnie shot a curious glance at Spencer through her eyelashes as they shared a pleasantly intimate dinner in the kitchen. She wanted to know more about him, and why he'd dropped into her lap at such an opportune moment. She was perfectly within her rights to ask him more about his background, at least about his work experience, but blatant inquisitiveness had never come easily to her.

She had to admit that Spencer had done an admirable job with dinner, though she could say without a doubt that he was not an experienced cook. She hadn't missed the way he'd mangled the eggs when he'd tried to crack them, or his clumsy way of handling the dinner-roll dough. He could follow directions well enough. The delicious roast her guests had enjoyed proved that. But she couldn't help suspecting that Spencer Guthrie was not the humble sociology student he claimed to be, seeking a job as a maid merely so he could pay his tuition and work in pleasant surroundings. No, he was hiding something.

"Did you get enough to eat?" Spencer asked her as he helped himself to another sliver of strawberry pie and a small dollop of whipped cream. "The meal wasn't half-bad."

"You sound as if you're surprised," Bonnie countered, concealing her amusement. "Frankly, the meal is exactly what I expected from someone with your qualifications."

Spencer looked warily at her for a moment, then eased into that smile Bonnie had already learned to anticipate. "Well, first-day-on-the-job jitters and all," he said by way of explanation. "So tell me, Bonnie, how did you break your ankle? Did you say something about falling off a ladder?''

"Yes, I was painting the trim when a big gust of—oh, no you don't," she said, realizing he'd handily changed the subject. "I've talked about myself and my hotel all evening. I want to know about you. Why did you really take this job? And if you don't give me a straight answer, I'll make you fill out those application forms I gave you earlier." She tried her best to sound like an authoritative employer.

Spencer shrugged, but the casual gesture didn't fool Bonnie. He was uneasy at the prospect of talking about himself. He wasn't shy, which left her back where she'd started. He was hiding something.

"I've told you all the important things," he said.

"Where are you from?" she asked, the challenge plain in the thrust of her chin.

"That's easy. Los Angeles."

"How did you end up in the great metropolis of Royal Springs, Arkansas? I would have thought you'd want to attend one of the excellent colleges in California."

"I was tired of California, particularly of the big city. I wanted to go somewhere with clean air, no traffic jams and friendly people. I ran across a brochure for the university here, and the decision to move just seemed to jell."

"But aren't you a little…mature to be a student? Not that I'm criticizing or anything—"

"Thirty-six is just entering the prime of life. Mature? You haven't hit thirty yet, or you wouldn't say such a thing."

Well, she'd stepped into that one. "I'm twenty-seven. But this is your job interview, remember?"

"You mean you're still not sure you want me, even after that spectacular dinner?" Spencer assumed just the correct air of self-righteous injury.

"There's more to being a maid than cooking." She ruined the stern effect of her words with a grin. "How do you feel about dishes?"

"Love 'em," was Spencer's reply. "I've always thought dishpan hands were sexy."

As if he needed any help in that department, Bonnie mused. "Well, you're going to have the sexiest hands in the Ozarks. The dishwasher's broken."

"Oh?"

She had to hand it to him. If he was distressed at the prospect of tackling a mountain of dishes by hand, he hid it well. "Theo says he can fix it tomorrow in time for the lunch dishes, providing the hardware store has the parts he needs." She slid off her stool, hobbled to the kitchen door and peeked into the dining room. Only a few guests remained, lingering over coffee. "You can clear the rest of the dishes now. I'll get the first sinkful going."

A few minutes later they stood side by side in front of the sink, Spencer washing and Bonnie drying as she leaned on one crutch for support. They talked easily now that Bonnie had dropped her inquisition, though sometimes they lapsed into silence and listened to the words of the country-and-western ballads playing on the old kitchen radio.

Bonnie couldn't remember when she'd enjoyed dirty dishes so much. Then again, she'd never before shared dishwater with a tall, firmly muscled male.

"You're slowing down," she teased him, reaching into the soapy sink to grab a dish. Their hands collided under the warm water, then lingered as each made a halfhearted attempt to get a grip on the slippery plate.

"Oops, I think I've got it now," Spencer said with a chuckle as he pulled the plate free of the water. He scrubbed it quickly, then handed it to Bonnie for rinsing and drying, their fingers brushing together once again.

The shivers that washed over Bonnie grew stronger with each inadvertent touch of his wet flesh on hers, until she could no longer ignore the signs of arousal. The realization was both familiar and, in some ways, totally new. It was only a normal, purely feminine physical reaction to Spencer's maleness, she tried to tell herself, but the growing intensity of her reaction to his nearness was disturbing, to say the least.

She was purposely careful over the next few minutes to keep her hands away from his.

Had he felt anything? she wondered. Or was the occasional accidental meeting of skin to skin an impersonal touch to him?

"Why don't you sit down and prop that leg up?" Spencer said as he began the last sinkful of dishes. "Your toes are turning purple."

Bonnie glanced down at her toes, protruding from the plaster cast, and decided they were an unhealthy shade. She'd been on her feet today far more than her doctor had recommended, and now she was paying for it with an aching leg.

"You're right," she said with a sigh, folding the damp dishcloth and laying it on the edge of the counter. "If you're sure everything's under control?"

"No problem."

"You'll wipe down the counters when you're through?"

"Yes. Now get yourself horizontal and rest."

"Hey, who's in charge here, anyway?" But she was warmed by Spencer's concern. Bonnie was assured she'd made the right decision in hiring him, regardless of his true motives for wanting the job. In fact, as pleasant as the prospect of lying down was, she felt reluctant to say good-night.

"I guess I'll see you in the—oh, wait." She reached into her pocket and extracted a gold key. "This is for the front door. You'll need to lock it on your way out."

She held the key out to him, then saw that both of his hands were covered with soapsuds. Without thinking, she slipped the key into his pants pocket instead, immediately regretting the action as she realized how close she'd come to making intimate contact.

She turned away hastily, before he could see the blush she was sure had overtaken her face. "See you tomorrow," she mumbled as she made her retreat.

Spencer stared after her, his body still reverberating from her touch. Damn! He'd almost swear she'd done it on purpose, except that knowing Bonnie even half a day, he'd come to realize she didn't have a flirtatious bone in her body. She hadn't intentionally rubbed her hands against his under the soapsuds, either, but the results were as effective as a purposeful seduction.

No, Bonnie's friendly manner was genuine, unaffected and utterly charming. And that's what made it so maddening. She didn't know the power of her own sensuality. She wasn't even trying to allure, yet somehow she was getting under his skin.

He finished up the dishes quickly, then wiped down the countertops, as promised. Satisfied that the kitchen was at least as clean as he'd found it, he turned out the lights, then made his way through the darkened dining room and into the lobby, where he paused to gaze at a fascinating sight. Bonnie sat halfway up the ornate flight of stairs, her long legs stretched out in front of her. She used her arms to haul herself up one step at a time, pausing between steps to drag her crutches with her.

"How do you ever expect to get to the top like that?" he asked, striding purposefully across the lobby. She was startled when she looked up, but then she lowered her eyes and smiled self-consciously.

"You weren't supposed to witness this indignity," she said, hardly noticing Spencer's slow ascent up the stairs. "And I've made it to the top like this four nights in a row. I just can't seem to get the hang of balancing myself on these crutches—Spencer, what do you think you're doing?" she sputtered as he leaned down and gathered her into his arms.

"I'm giving you a lift," he replied, noting that Bonnie made a surprisingly light burden, even with the cast to weigh her down. As he carried her to the top, the scent of her hair, or maybe it was her skin, reminded him of the small purple mountain flowers that flourished everywhere in Royal Springs. He inhaled deeply, closing his eyes for a moment. When he opened them, Bonnie's gray-green eyes, fringed with surprisingly dark lashes for one so fair, stared up at him in an expression of either disapproval or amusement—he couldn't decipher which.

"This is not part of your job description," she said as he deposited her gently at the top of the stairs.

"Consider it service above and beyond the call of duty." He bounded halfway down the stairs with more energy than the circumstances warranted, retrieved Bonnie's crutches, and returned them to her, wondering why he couldn't eradicate the ridiculous smile he could feel on his face. He was acting like an idiot, babbling silly clichés that wouldn't do justice to a hormone-driven teenager.

But there was something about Bonnie, a certain sense of helplessness, perhaps, that had awakened a primitive protective instinct inside Spencer. No matter how hard he tried to deny its existence, or rationalize it away, the instinct was undeniably there. Curious.

"Need anything else before I go?" he asked in an almost-even voice.

"No, thanks."

The shy smile she flashed just before turning away nearly undid him.

Spencer made his escape before he could say or do anything else foolish, hoping the cool mountain air would clear his head as he bicycled back to his apartment. Physical attraction at first sight was something he believed in. It had happened to him often enough over the years, and it was something he seldom worried about. Either things worked out or they didn't. But this mind-bending emotional reaction, which had descended upon him almost from the moment he'd met Bonnie, was a new experience.

"Women are not helpless," he said aloud as he mounted his ten-speed and pushed off. "Women are strong. They can take care of themselves. Women don't need men to take care of them." He continued to murmur such sentiments all the way home. The words were comforting.

Bonnie made a conscious effort to relax her muscles as she lay in her massive four-poster, but once again sleep eluded her. Ever since her accident, the cumbersome cast had made a nuisance of itself during the night. Once it had fallen over the edge of the bed and dragged Bonnie with it.

Tonight, however, the uncomfortable cast was only part of her problem. More troubling by far were feelings that came from within, feelings that had taken root from the time Spencer Guthrie's voice had startled her that afternoon.

Years had passed since she'd felt anything approaching attraction for a man. And such attraction! Never had she come face-to-face with such striking evidence of her own womanhood. Desire had never before reared its head so suddenly, and Bonnie wasn't sure if she knew how to handle it.

The first seeds of worry had been planted the moment Spencer had scooped her into his arms, when she'd sensed a hint of answering desire in him. That's the part that scared her.

As long as her feelings were one-sided, they were safe. But now that she knew Spencer felt something, too, her own desires moved out of the realm of fantasy and into an arena of possibilities.

Pulling the pillow over her head, she groaned at the direction in which her thoughts traveled. It was late, she was tired, and her imagination was running amok. She was reading too much into the situation. Spencer had helped her up the stairs because he was a friendly, helpful person. She'd reacted to his proximity because she was a healthy woman. That didn't mean a blessed thing.

Chapter Three

Now that the Rose Garden Room was actually his personal domicile, Spencer didn't think it was funny. He was sure that by the end of the summer he would hate pink with a passion.

His first instinct that morning, when he'd moved a few belongings into the maid's quarters, had been to pull down the ruffled canopy and frilly curtains. But upon reflection he'd decided to leave the room as it was—if only to remind him of his goal at the Sweetwater Inn. He was here to observe, to broaden his experiences and to add to his body of knowledge about stereotyped sex roles.

His goal did not include a romantic liaison with his employer, he told himself that afternoon as he stepped into the shower. But even the thought of her caused muscles to tighten and breath to shorten. He turned the cold-water faucet on high.

He was combing his sandy hair into some semblance of order when a buzzer above the door sounded. He looked up, surprised. How Victorian. A bell to summon the servant.

He leaned his head out the door. "Be right there," he called, shoving his arms hastily into the sleeves of a clean white shirt, simultaneously sliding his feet into loafers.

When he reached the lobby, he saw why he'd been called. Two guests were signing the register, and they'd brought with them an inordinate amount of luggage.

Bonnie greeted him with a cheerful wave, as she often did, and Spencer's heart did its habitual flip-flop at the sight of her smile. Who could remain unaffected? he rationalized. She was dazzling.

"This is Mr. and Mrs. Hoskins," Bonnie said. "Spencer, could you take their bags to Room 203?"

"Sure." Spencer turned his attention to the couple for the first time, and the smile froze on his face. Randy Hoskins and Jenny Sands. Neither student acknowledged him, but Jenny's mouth was pursed in silent amusement and Randy was chewing on his lip to keep from laughing.

When Spencer picked up the first suitcase, he knew he was in for a helluva weekend. The bag had to be filled with rocks. When he tested one of the other bags, it was just as heavy. With grim determination he picked up the first bag with two hands and proceeded up the stairs.

"All right, what are you two up to?" Spencer said as he heaved the final suitcase onto a luggage rack, which sagged under the bag's weight.

Jenny twisted a tendril of her carrot-red hair and assumed an expression of innocence. "Why, nothing! When you described this place, it just sounded so nice we thought we'd try it out for the weekend. Where's your apron, Professor?"

"You'll see it at dinner," Spencer replied between clenched teeth. "Now, look, kiddies, if you're here to give me a hard time, that's fine. But if Bonnie—Mrs. Chapman finds out I'm anything but on the level she'll probably fire me. This situation is turning out to be an invaluable opportunity for research, so you'd better not blow my cover. Got that?"

"Sure, no problem," said Randy.

Spencer did not feel reassured as he started dinner. Something ominous was in the air, and for once he wished he wasn't so friendly with his students. He didn't intimidate the kids in the slightest. Consequently he was a convenient target for practical jokes.

Preparing the meat loaf from Bonnie's recipe was fairly easy; the fried potatoes and steamed broccoli with cheese sauce were a snap. Then Randy and Jenny went into their song and dance, and dinner went downhill from there.

From the salad to the dessert, Jenny's food was unsatisfactory. Could she have a salad *without* mushrooms, please? Didn't the Sweetwater Inn have any low-cal dressing? The potatoes weren't done enough; then they were too done. The meat loaf needed catsup, the cheese sauce was too thick. Even dessert, Bonnie's award-winning devil's food cake, required an extra glass of milk because it was too sweet.

When Jenny wasn't making some ridiculous demand, Randy was spilling or dropping something: water, tea, silverware, napkins.

It was an evening Spencer wouldn't soon forget. When all of the guests were finally gone and Spencer's juggling act was over for the evening, he felt a tremendous sense of relief. It was only with the utmost skill that he had maintained composure, barely squelching the urge to drop some gloppy food into Jenny's lap.

"All right, Spencer, what's going on?" Bonnie demanded as they sat down to their own dinner in the kitchen.

Spencer had more or less expected the question, but he disliked it anyway. This was the first time Bonnie had shown any real displeasure toward him. "Is something wrong?" he asked innocently.

"The way you were stomping in and out of the dining room, how could I not notice something was wrong? One of our guests is a troublemaker, is that it?"

"Two troublemakers, actually, but I took care of them—tactfully. You don't have to wrinkle your nose at me like that."

Bonnie let the matter drop, but she knew instinctively that Spencer wasn't telling her the whole story. She couldn't help watching him with scarcely disguised curiosity as she helped him load the dishwasher. Though he'd regained much of his cheerfulness, he still maintained a certain edge of tension, evident in his every move.

She should try to get to the bottom of this mystery. And yet she hesitated, not wishing to rock the boat. Spencer was turning out to be a very good maid after all. He wasn't particularly skilled at domestic tasks, but what he lacked in experience he made up for with effort and enthusiasm. He also exhibited a range of talents no female housekeeper could possess. He was strong enough to unstick any window and tall enough to change any light bulb, not to mention that he was easier on her eyes than the woman with the tattoo would have been.

Yes, she liked the way his shirt pulled tight across his broad shoulders as he struggled with the stubborn dishwasher soap dispenser. She liked the determined set of his square jaw, and the way his thick sandy hair curled defiantly into several cowlicks, softening his otherwise imposing good looks. She liked his graceful stride as he returned to the dining room to gather the last few coffee cups. Where would she ever find another maid who fulfilled those qualifications?

When he disappeared into the dining room she sighed, realizing she hadn't embellished a single thing about him in her wild imaginings the other night. She was sharing her roof with an exceptionally good-looking man and fighting a strong physical and emotional reaction to him. Every time their eyes met, even for the most innocent of conversations, she saw her own desire mirrored there.

Where, if anywhere, did things go from here?

By late Sunday night Spencer's body was stressed out. His muscles ached from all the bending and stretching his new job required, his hands were chapped and his knees were sore. He was also tense from handling one near-disaster after another for the entire weekend. Randy and Jenny had eased up on him after the novelty of seeing him in an apron had worn off, but that still left the cooking, cleaning and laundry. In between tasks, he was skillfully shielding Bonnie from his occasional lapses in expertise.

The students had left a few hours ago. The inn was peaceful, devoid of guests except for an elderly couple who were so quiet Spencer scarcely knew they were there. He couldn't think of a more perfect time to try out the mineral baths. If anyone's body and spirit needed healing, it was his.

As he changed into swimming trunks, he was acutely aware of Bonnie's closeness. Although his responsibilities did not include cleaning her room, he knew that her quarters were situated directly over his. He had heard her last night, moving about on her crutches as she prepared for bed, and the knowledge that mere wood and plaster separated them as they slept had accelerated his heartbeat for sleepless hours on end.

Tonight was no better. He'd made a preliminary attempt to fall asleep but couldn't seem to get comfortable, no matter which way he contorted himself. He sincerely hoped those warm mineral waters would live up to their claims.

Maybe when he became accustomed to Bonnie's constant presence, she wouldn't affect him so strongly, he reasoned as he made his way along the covered walkway that connected the main building to the bathhouse. But that, he knew, was utter nonsense. With the passing of time his responses grew stronger, not weaker.

The bathhouse was a study in Victorian ostentation. The stonework inside and out, though crumbling in places, was fraught with curlicues, gargoyles, grapes and flowers. Ceramic tiles formed an intricate mosaic on the floor, and reproductions of Greek statues looked down from their wall niches at the bathing pools.

Spencer had his choice of three pools, each a different temperature and filled with a slightly different variety of water. He didn't bother to read the brass plaques that lauded the benefits of each particular bath, he just sought out the warmest pool and eased himself in with a sigh. This was going to be heaven.

He sat on one of the benches carved into the sides of the pool. Soaking in steaming water up to his chin, he leaned his head back on the stone ledge and closed his eyes. He allowed each thought to drift as it pleased until chaos began to assume a logical order. Gradually his mind emptied and his facial muscles relaxed as the sound of trickling water lulled him into an uncomplicated sleep.

Bonnie was determined to enjoy a mineral bath, though she had no idea how she would accomplish this feat without getting her cast wet. But even if she could just dangle her good leg in the pool and listen to the relaxing sound of swirling, gurgling water, she was sure it would relieve her fatigue and help her get to sleep.

Sleep. The shortage she'd experienced this week was catching up to her. Just when she was getting used to the discomfort of the cast, she had discovered she still couldn't sleep soundly. Spencer Guthrie's image invaded her dreams, causing her to awaken with a racing heart and adrenaline pumping by the gallon through her veins.

When she reached the bathhouse, she was surprised to discover the light was on. She made a mental note to remind Theo, who cleaned and maintained the bathhouse, to be more careful about turning off lights. She was no longer scraping for every penny, but she still could scarcely afford to pay unnecessarily high electric bills.

The smallest bath, which as children she, Sammy and Kenny had dubbed the Lover's Pool, seemed the easiest to navigate. She moved carefully across the slick tile toward the small concrete depression, which was tucked into an alcove and surrounded by ivy and stone representations of cupids and doves.

"Colonel, you must have been a romantic old devil," she said aloud as she contemplated how best to approach the water.

"What?"

She whirled around so suddenly that she almost lost her footing and fell into the pool. "Spencer! Lord, you scared the living daylights out of me."

"Sorry." He sat up straighter and splashed water into his face. "You startled me, too. I'm afraid I dozed off."

"It's a good thing I found you, then. If you'd slept there all night, in the morning there might have been nothing left but a shrunken prune." She pulled her terry robe more tightly around her. If she'd thought anyone else would be about, particularly Spencer, she would have worn something less revealing than her French-cut black bikini.

"What are you doing here, anyway?" Spencer asked. "I thought you couldn't get your cast wet."

Bonnie sighed. "I can't. I just thought maybe I could figure out a way to get everything *but* the cast wet." She lowered herself carefully to the edge of the pool, stretching the cast out in front of her and dangling her other leg in the warm water. "This is probably the best I can do."

"Nonsense. You just need an extra hand, that's all."

Spencer hoisted himself out of the water, then walked toward her, reminding Bonnie of nothing so much as Poseidon rising from the sea. Poseidon in a ridiculously brief swimsuit. She resisted the urge to avert her eyes.

The confident grin spreading across his face did not put her at ease.

"Just what did you have in mind?" she asked, knowing that whatever it was it would require bodily contact, which would completely negate the relaxing effect of the hot bath.

"Just a little experiment."

Her apprehension increased as she caught a whiff of Spencer's soapy-clean scent and felt the heat from his body. He was close enough now to touch. Could she possibly back out at this point? Not without raising too many questions. She removed her terry robe with a slight shiver as Spencer slid into the waist-deep pool.

"Just turn your back toward the water and lean into me," he directed, placing his hands on her shoulders from behind. Bonnie tensed at his first touch, but his hands were warm and reassuring, not threatening in any way. She found herself relaxing as she followed his directions, shifting her weight into his arms. He lowered her gently into the warm water until only her lower legs remained dry, supported on the pool ledge.

"I told you this would work." Spencer stood beside her, holding her in the water with one hand at her shoulders, his forearm supporting her head, and the other at the small of her back. "Comfortable?"

"Mmm-hmm." This *was* comfortable, she decided, taking in the excellent view of Spencer's pectorals. It was also utterly ridiculous. How could she relax with all those hard muscles in such close proximity? She was acutely aware of the position of his hands, the exact placement of his fingers on her shoulder blades and at the base of her spine.

"What about you?" she asked after a few moments, looking up into his golden eyes. "Are you comfortable?" She took a deep breath, knowing she should look away from the blatant hunger she saw there, but unable to. She was in danger of drowning—not in the pool, but in the depths of her own sudden desire, which was mirrored so plainly in Spencer's gaze.

"I'm comfortable in some ways," he responded, never taking his eyes away from hers. "I'd feel better if you'd relax, though."

"I am relaxed." The words came out much more shrilly than she intended.

"Try putting your arms around my neck."

"I don't—"

"You'll put less strain on your back that way."

They were playing a game and Bonnie knew it. Still she couldn't make herself resist. Tentatively she moved her arms around Spencer's neck, reveling in the slippery feel of water against his smooth skin.

"Better, right?"

Bonnie nodded uncertainly as his hands began to move under the warm water, exploring her back and shoulders in a leisurely fashion. He toyed with the bow that fastened her swimsuit top in back, but a stern warning look from Bonnie stilled his hand.

The corner of his mouth drew up in a mischievous half smile. He leaned closer to her, one inch at a time.

My Lord, he's going to kiss me, Bonnie thought as her breathing accelerated. *I should do something.* She became aware of a vague warmth emanating from deep within her. The warmth spread from her core to her limbs, and into her fingers and toes, paralyzing her with pleasurable sensations.

Spencer's smile disappeared as he came closer still, replaced by an expression of determined intent as his lips closed over hers.

If she was going to object, Bonnie thought dazedly, she should have done it long before this. Now she felt powerless under the assault of his mesmerizing kiss, which seemed to give of everything and ask for everything in return. She was thankful her arms were firmly anchored around his neck, for she could have easily slid under the water, drowned and never known the difference.

"You are sweet, Bonnie Chapman," Spencer murmured against her lips. She leaned her head back and let the warm water claim her long hair as Spencer's lips moved to the sensitive hollow of her throat.

New and crazy sensations were hurtling through Bonnie's body. She couldn't put a name to the feelings, but she knew this was like nothing she'd experienced before. She wound her fingers into Spencer's thick, damp hair, inhaled his tantalizing scent. She trembled as his lips traced a delicate pattern against her neck and along her jaw, finally returning to her mouth.

"You must be part witch." He scarcely breathed the words. "How else can you explain this, this..." He paused, apparently searching for the right word. He never finished the sentence.

"This what?" Bonnie asked, longing to hear his thoughts.

The question remained unanswered as Spencer kissed her again. His tongue sought entrance to her mouth as his fingers brushed the side of her breast. She felt her nipples tightening in a surge of pure excitement, and she pulled him closer still as her body demanded more.

"Let me carry you upstairs and make love to you," he whispered against her ear.

Those were not words Bonnie had expected, not at all.

At the same moment that Spencer realized he'd spoken his thoughts aloud, he felt Bonnie stiffen and knew he'd made a mistake.

"I don't think this was a good idea," Bonnie said, her voice shaking slightly. "Help me out of the water."

Spencer complied with her wishes, seeing no other choice. He longed to let his hands linger against her smooth skin after he'd set her safely on the pool ledge, but he fully recognized that the fiery sparks in her eyes no longer had anything to do with desire. She'd been kissing him with all the reserve of molten lava, yet when he'd mentioned the prospect of further intimacy, she'd frozen into a glacier.

Pulling himself out of the water, he sat next to her, his legs still dangling in the pool, as Bonnie blotted the moisture from her face and arms with her terry robe.

"I said the wrong thing," he finally offered.

"Yes, you did." She wouldn't look directly at him, but he caught a hint of hurt or perhaps disappointment in her eyes.

"You're feeling disloyal to your husband, is that it?"

Her head jerked up, and she stared at him as if he'd grown another nose. "What on God's green earth does Sammy have to do with this?"

Spencer shrugged, relieved that he was wrong but still perplexed by Bonnie's sudden hostility. "I just thought ... could you at least give me a clue?"

This time when she looked at him, her narrowed eyes were as dark and murky as polished jade. "I don't know what you're accustomed to, but in my book two people don't make love unless they're *in* love, and certainly not after a few days' acquaintance. I'm insulted by your casual suggestion—that is, unless you meant it as a compliment to suggest that I have the morals of an alley cat."

Her words had the effect of a slap. "I didn't mean to insult you."

Bonnie sighed, a long, deep sigh that reached inside Spencer and shook his soul. "Let's just forget this, okay? If you meant no insult, I'll take you at your word. But from now on I expect you to act like an employee, not some Casanova."

She stood with as much dignity as her cumbersome cast would allow, then exited the bathhouse, leaving Spencer to stare after her in consternation.

He felt an honest desire for Bonnie, and he'd put it into words. There was nothing wrong with that—women were always saying they wanted honesty in their relationships. They didn't want games; they didn't expect to be coaxed into bed. The decision to make love was supposed to be a mutual one that afforded pleasure to both partners.

That was what the studies and surveys said, and many of his female colleagues had supported this evidence with their own opinions.

Why, then, did he feel so wretchedly guilty?

Perhaps it was impossible to quantify and average such intimate subjects, he mused. Anyway, how could he expect a unique woman such as Bonnie to fit neatly into the statistical mold of the "modern woman" that sociology had shaped?

He was learning that Bonnie was a woman of uncommonly traditional values—a member of an endangered species, based on what he heard and what he knew from personal experience. Given that, Spencer's proposition had been entirely inappropriate, and he *should* feel guilty.

He shook his head at the futility of his position. He wanted Bonnie with an intensity that shook him to his core, yet how could things possibly work between them? They held two divergent philosophies, and tonight's incident illustrated that fact all too well. She was a genteel Southern belle who dreamed of love and long-term commitment; the idea of permanence scared him to death. She wanted a man to woo her with hearts and flowers; he simply didn't know how to be that kind of man. Their differing needs could never meld.

Bonnie was feeling decidedly contrite as she grated cheese for omelets the next morning. She'd lain awake for hours after leaving Spencer, wondering exactly what had motivated her sudden spurt of self-righteous indignation. Had she actually been offended by Spencer's suggestion? Or was her tersely delivered response merely a self-preservational tactic, brought on by the shock of her own wanton response to his kisses?

She could have simply turned down his proposal, instead of making that puritanical-sounding speech. Then again, by staging a strong, indignant reaction, she'd effectively turned off the frighteningly intense heat in her own body, as well as his. A simple no might not have accomplished this.

"The cheese is ready," she said, holding the bowl out to Spencer like a peace offering. They'd hardly exchanged two words this morning, limiting their conversation to only what was essential.

Spencer took the bowl with a muttered "thanks," then returned his attention to the butter melting in two omelet pans.

"Spencer, about last night—"

He turned toward her abruptly. "Please, don't say it. I know I was a jerk. I was way out of line and I apologize."

Bonnie was taken aback by Spencer's sudden penitence. She'd mistaken his silence this morning for anger, but perhaps, like her, he felt confused and embarrassed about the whole incident.

She managed a smile. "Your apology is accepted. And your butter is burning."

Spencer whirled around and removed the smoking pans from the stove. "Is there any chance, Bonnie, that I can persuade you to take over these omelets? I think I'm ready to admit that I'm not *quite* the cook you are."

"Of course I'll fix the omelets." Bonnie sighed with relief as she maneuvered herself off the stool and reached for her crutches. Perhaps the subject of the previous evening was closed, and things could get back to normal.

The state of normalcy lasted exactly two hours.

After breakfast, Theo drove Bonnie into town to run errands. The inn was quiet, so Spencer decided to grade some test papers while minding the front desk and the phone.

He worked for more than an hour, interrupted only by Marmalade, the inn's big orange cat, who every so often awoke from his nap on the desk to bat playfully at the end of Spencer's pen. The inn was so calm, in fact, that when a flashy young man plowed through the front door with all the finesse of a tornado, the interruption was doubly disturbing.

"Well!" the man said, taking a turn about the lobby with an eager eye. "This place hasn't changed a bit. Where's Bonnie?"

Spencer took in the man's appearance with a good once-over, instinctively not liking what he saw. The clothes were ultrastylish, obviously expensive; the cut of the man's blond hair was definitely avant-garde. He was *too* handsome.

"Mrs. Chapman isn't in at the moment," Spencer said, carefully neutral. "Can I help you?"

"Well, well, don't tell me Bonnie's gone and hired herself a manager?"

"I'm just filling in," said Spencer, realizing with some surprise that he was embarrassed to admit to this arrogant stranger that he was actually the housekeeper. He'd have to add that to his notes later. "What can I do for you?" It was more of a demand than a polite question.

The stranger, to Spencer's immense irritation, still didn't introduce himself or offer any explanation for his presence. Instead he ambled closer to the registration desk, extending one negligent hand toward the sleeping cat.

The cat awoke, hissing disdainfully.

"Now, Clotilde, you remember me, don't you, girl?"

"I believe the cat's name is Marmalade," Spencer said coolly.

"Oh, well, Clotilde must have gone to the happy hunting ground. She was getting on when I last saw her—five years ago. Look, when do you expect Bonnie to return?"

Five years ago. That was a very familiar-sounding time period, Spencer thought as a nasty suspicion entered his thoughts. He was just about to answer the man when the front door opened again, admitting Bonnie and Theo.

"Whew, it's hot out there," Bonnie said as she looked down at her feet while negotiating the two steps that led down to the lobby. "Any problems, Spencer?"

"I'll say," he mumbled, not even bothering to conceal his test papers. He figured no one would notice them during the next few minutes.

Bonnie reached the bottom of the steps and looked up questioningly. When her eyes fell on the stranger, the color seemed to drain from her face until she was as pale as the plaster cast on her leg.

Theo, too, seemed to have been rendered speechless as he stared at their visitor.

When Bonnie finally found her voice, her words came out in a faint croak. "Kenny Chapman, is that really you?"

Chapter Four

Bonnie thought she was going to faint. She'd heard of people passing out from shock, but she'd never done it herself. Only Theo's steadying hand at her elbow prevented her sudden dizziness from causing her to topple head over heels into the lobby.

"Bonnie, my little Bonnie Sue! You look just as pretty as I remembered—prettier even." Kenny's greeting was strident and cheerful. "But what on earth happened to your leg?"

"Who cares what happened to me!" Bonnie shouted as the light-headedness abated and a giddy laugh took its place. Kenny came forward, enveloping her in an over-enthusiastic bear hug. She returned it in kind, relieved beyond words to see him alive and well. "I thought you were dead," she said, swallowing back tears.

"Nah, I'm too tough to go without a fight," he reassured her.

After a moment, however, Bonnie's joy and relief were joined by a healthy dose of outrage. "I thought you were dead!" she repeated in a sharper voice, pulling out of his embrace. "Five years and no word? You couldn't have made a phone call? Written a postcard? *Something?*"

"Bonnie, Bonnie, you can scold me later," he said, keeping hold of both her hands. "Right now I just want to drink in the sight of you."

Over Kenny's shoulder, Bonnie saw Spencer stand up from behind the registration desk, an unreadable expression on his face. "I won't intrude," he said quickly just as Bonnie was about to make introductions. "I'm sure the two of you have a lot to catch up on, and I have some laundry to take care of. Bonnie," he added, "your toes are turning purple again." He made a brisk exit.

Theo, after quickly shaking Kenny's hand and offering a hesitant "Welcome home," followed Spencer.

"Spencer's my new housekeeper," Bonnie explained as she heeded his warning about her toes and sank into the nearest chair, propping up her leg.

Kenny looked momentarily confused. "You mean, like a concierge?"

She didn't know exactly what a concierge was, but she was fairly certain Spencer wasn't one. "No, I mean like a housekeeper. You know, sweeping, cooking, laundry?"

Kenny threw his head back and laughed. "You're kidding. You hired a man for a maid?"

"What's wrong with that?" she asked sharply, though just a few days ago she'd been of the same frame of mind. "Besides, I had to hire someone. I couldn't keep doing all the work myself, not with this cast on my leg."

"Oh, so this is a temporary deal, till you're healed up." Kenny looked much relieved as he sat in the love seat across from her.

"Maybe. You know, I've been running the inn by myself for a long time. I must say it's nice to have some help around here for a change."

"Oh, I plan to help out a lot," he said, smiling confidently. "I guess I picked a good time to come back."

Bonnie tried to pick up the smile she'd lost a few moments ago, but didn't succeed. She wanted some answers. The prodigal son had returned, but she was far from ready to bring on the fatted calf, even if she'd had one. "Exactly where is it you're coming back from?" she asked pointedly.

"France, Spain, Portugal. I wandered around quite a bit."

"And what were you doing?"

"A little of this, a little of that."

"Kenny Chapman, is that all you have to say for five years of your life?"

At that, he looked away from her, obviously uneasy, which struck Bonnie as odd. Kenny was never uneasy. "I'm not proud of the way I lived most of those five years," he said quietly. "I left here vowing to make something of myself. Instead I talked too much, drank too much. I ultimately ended up in jail. That's why I never wrote you back, Bonnie. I was too ashamed of myself."

She felt immediately contrite. Poor Kenny. He'd always been so sure he could conquer the world. "Kenny, didn't you know you'd always be welcomed back here? You're family, after all. And this is your home."

Kenny's smile returned. "I should have known I could count on you, Bonnie. But don't waste a minute feeling sorry for me. It took a while, but I got my life straightened out. From a chance meeting I finagled a job in a textile factory. And from there—you do know what textiles are, don't you?''

"Yes—fabric and such, right?''

He nodded. "I discovered I had a talent for it, and pretty soon I moved into the design end. I was an up-and-comer.''

"And?''

Kenny shrugged. "I started making money, enough to afford some decent clothes and a fancy apartment. I was living pretty high. And then I ran across a couple of your old letters. I started thinking about you, all alone here. Suddenly the money and the status didn't mean as much.''

Bonnie felt even more guilty for her earlier, less charitable thoughts. The family did mean something to Kenny, after all.

"Have you seen your mom?'' she asked.

"Yeah, I stopped in Miami first. She's older than I remembered. She, uh, she sends her love.''

Bonnie wagged an admonishing finger at her brother-in-law. "Now, Kenny, you know she did nothing of the kind. If she'd sent anything it would have been curses.''

Kenny grinned sheepishly. "All right, you caught me. I just hate to believe that things are so grim between you two. I knew she didn't approve of Sam's marrying you, but I had no idea she was so bitter.''

"She's more bitter about Sammy's death than the marriage,'' Bonnie explained. "I think she'd like to blame someone, and I'm her most logical choice. But let's not talk about that,'' she said briskly. "We have so much else to catch up on. How long are you planning to stay?''

There was a long pause. "I hadn't planned on leaving again at all," he said, his voice full of earnestness. "The Sweetwater Inn is my legacy from my father. I owe it to him to see you through these hard times and get the inn back on its feet again."

"But these aren't hard times," Bonnie objected. "Of course, I'm delighted to have your help, but the inn is operating in the black."

"But in your last letter you said things were really tough, that you almost had to close down."

"Lord, Kenny, that was more than three years ago! Haven't you received any letters since then?"

Kenny shook his head.

"Well, for your information the Sweetwater Inn is in very good shape."

Kenny smiled brightly. "Fortunes have turned around for the inn, huh? And you're making a profit? Why, Bonnie, how lucky for you." He leaned across the gap separating them and squeezed her shoulder in a congratulatory gesture.

"Lucky... yes, I suppose I was." She tapped her cast with one fingernail. "Then again—"

"And now I'm here," Kenny continued, cutting her off. "So you won't have to carry the responsibility of managing this place alone, not ever again."

For years Bonnie had longed to hear those reassuring words from someone. Responsibility for the hotel could be a heavy burden sometimes. Even though Theo often lent a sympathetic ear, and occasionally a shoulder to cry on, she'd often felt so alone.

She placed one of her hands over Kenny's. "You can't imagine how relieved I am that you're here to stay."

But already Kenny was scarcely listening. "Yeah, I think this place could be a real gold mine," he said as he pulled away from her, thoughtfully eyeing the lobby furnishings. "The showpiece of the whole town—maybe even the whole state."

Spencer stood at the top of the basement stairs with an arm load of clean sheets, shamelessly eavesdropping. Normally he wouldn't stoop to such measures, but his instincts told him there was trouble afoot. He hadn't liked or trusted Kenny Chapman from the moment the man had oozed through the front door, and the more he heard Kenny talk, the more he was sure his instincts were on the money.

So Kenny thought the inn was in trouble, and he'd felt compelled to leave a comfortable situation and come to the rescue? What a bunch of malarkey! More than likely, Ken had purposely stayed away when the inn was experiencing lean times, and had returned only when he was sure he wouldn't be held responsible for any losses.

But how could Ken have known? He'd been out of touch, and out of the country, for five years.

Spencer reconsidered. Was he letting personal feelings get in the way of reason? *Admit it, Guthrie, you're envious of the little worm.* Ken had known Bonnie his whole life; they shared a long history and a familial tie that made Spencer feel shut out.

"Now, how ridiculous is that?" he murmured to himself as he headed upstairs with the sheets. Bonnie's relationship with her brother-in-law was none of his concern. He vowed that he would give Ken Chapman the benefit of the doubt, instincts or no.

Over the next few days, however, Spencer's initial suspicions were confirmed. Ken Chapman was a male chauvinist and a manipulator, pure and simple, and Bonnie, so sweet and trusting, fell for his line of bull.

It was all Spencer could do not to interfere. His professional side was fascinated by the dynamics between those two. He observed them carefully and made conscientious notes to add to his storehouse of knowledge about gender roles. On a more personal level, however, observing them made him want to do something. He constantly had to tamp down his outrage and remind himself that he was here as an observer, not an instigator of social reform.

Bonnie thoughtfully fingered the collar of her plain cotton nightgown before folding the garment and laying it in her overnight case.

Spending the weekend in Little Rock had seemed like a good idea yesterday, when she'd decided to make the trip. Literally years had passed since she'd gotten away from the inn for some time to herself. Instead she was feeling guilty about abandoning the homestead.

She should have been excited about the shopping spree she'd planned. Just lately she'd become aware of the deplorable state of her wardrobe—especially her lingerie, she thought as she dropped two pairs of panties, the serviceable cotton variety, into the suitcase. She made a mental note to replace them with some silk and satin numbers in a rainbow of pastel hues, a thought that cheered her somewhat.

She told herself for the umpteenth time to stop worrying. Kenny had been here almost two weeks and was settling into a routine. He was competent enough to handle the hotel for one weekend. He really seemed enthusiastic about running the inn, and this past week he'd dived into each task with boundless energy, making a host of suggestions for improvements.

She had to admit that a few of Kenny's ideas were workable. He'd been halfway to an M.B.A. before quitting school, and he knew more about taxes and how to avoid them than Bonnie ever would. On the other hand, her five years at the helm had taught her a great deal about the day-to-day dealings of the hotel—things Kenny needed to learn.

Their talents should have complemented each other. But instead she found herself more and more often at odds with her brother-in-law. And though he was couching his ideas in terms of helpful suggestions right now, she recognized that before long he would begin to exert his authority as a fifty-percent partner in the business. Final decisions would be taken out of her hands. She only hoped that he would wait until he knew the situation before he tried to take the reins.

Kenny wasn't her only worry. There was also Spencer.

Bonnie sank onto the edge of her bed, the packing forgotten for the moment. Spencer wasn't comfortable around Kenny—that was plain.

She sighed quietly as she pictured him in her mind, and the way he'd smiled and teased the first couple of days they'd worked together. Easygoing, friendly, talkative Spencer had transformed himself into a veritable sphinx over the past several days. She couldn't fault his work. He was becoming more competent by the day. But he hadn't uttered more than a couple of words to anyone since Kenny's arrival.

She wasn't sure if his reticence was entirely due to Kenny's unsettling presence; she was forced to admit that he might still be smarting from the rebuke she'd given him the night he'd kissed her. Whatever, she intended to find out what the problem was. She'd had enough of him sneaking around the inn like a thief, seeming to disappear around a corner every time she entered a room.

Closing the small suitcase, she zipped it shut. Then she threw the strap over her shoulder, picked up her crutches and headed out her bedroom door. She found Spencer just where she expected, sweeping the hallway with quiet efficiency.

"Spencer? Would you mind carrying my bag out to the truck? It's not heavy, but I have enough trouble getting just myself down the stairs."

Spencer immediately set his broom aside. "Sure, I'd be happy to." He took the bag and her crutches, then offered his arm.

Bonnie tried not to notice the feel of that strong arm, the way the muscles flexed beneath her hand as he tensed them to support her. She'd nearly forgotten what his nearness did to her.

She hadn't been this close to Spencer since the fateful mineral bath incident, except in her overactive imagination. Once or twice, when she'd let her guard down, she'd relived those intimate moments they'd shared in the bathhouse, letting the fantasy proceed to a different conclusion each time. If she could rewrite the scene, would she? Would she ever get the chance to orchestrate a different scene altogether?

Shaking herself back into reality, Bonnie said quick goodbyes to Theo and Kenny, then insisted that Spencer carry her bag all the way out to the carport at the back of the hotel.

He set the overnight case into the bed of Bonnie's small truck, eyeing it skeptically. "Are you sure that one little bag will get you through three whole days?" he asked.

Bonnie leaned against Theo's ancient white sedan, parked in the slot next to the truck. "I'm going shopping as soon as I leave the doctor's office this afternoon. If I need any more clothes I'll buy them.''

"But how can you maneuver through a shopping center with a broken ankle?''

"I checked with the mall. They have some motorized carts for people like me.''

"And you're sure you can handle the truck?''

"It's an automatic." She had to smile at Spencer's sudden concern. He hadn't voiced any objections yesterday when she'd announced her intention to make the weekend trip, but she thought she'd noticed a flash of disapproval cross his face. She was gratified that he wasn't letting her go without a few misgivings.

"But you won't hesitate to call if you need anything?" he said.

"I'll be fine," she reassured once again as she opened the driver's door of her compact pickup. She sat on the edge of the seat, then paused. "Spencer," she said slowly, "are you worried about me? Or are you worried about me leaving Kenny in charge?"

Spencer sighed. "Both. How could I not be? And if I were you, I'd be worried, too. Your brother-in-law—" He stopped himself.

So, Spencer did share her concern. Still, she felt obligated to turn a confident face forward. "I know Kenny has some strange ideas, but you have to remember he's had a lot more formal business education than either of us. He's been places and seen things I've only dreamed of. His way of doing things might be different from mine, but I'm no expert in business management. Besides, I think you and Kenny will get on much better without me looking over your shoulders."

A decidedly guilty expression crossed Spencer's finely chiseled features, but he made no reply.

"You're not exactly friendly toward Kenny, you know," she continued. "At least Kenny's made an effort to talk to you. Why don't you try talking back?"

"Oh, but Ken doesn't expect me to talk back," he explained with mock seriousness. "I'm just the *maid*, after all."

"Hmm, yes, I know what you mean." Bonnie rubbed her forehead as she thought about that. "He does have a somewhat lord-of-the-manor attitude, even toward me. It's pretty hard to swallow sometimes. But..." she paused, deciding whether she really wanted to go on with her next thought.

"But what?"

"Just because you're aloof with Ken doesn't mean you can't still talk to me."

"What do you mean?" he asked, all innocence. "I talk to you. I'm talking to you now."

"This is the first conversation we've had all week," she said softly. "And you're only here because I practically ordered you to carry my bag out—as if I couldn't have handled it by myself."

Spencer knew he was guilty as charged. In truth it had been a struggle to keep his lip buttoned over the past several days. But if he'd opened his mouth once, just once, he would have told Bonnie what he thought about Ken Chapman. And he doubted that would have earned many points with her.

"Those first couple of days you were at the inn we talked all the time," Bonnie continued. "Here, lately I can't get you to put two words together."

He didn't miss the crack in her voice. The last thing he'd meant to do was hurt her feelings. "It's nothing you've done, Bonnie," he hurried to say.

"Oh? Then what is it?"

"It's...it's Ken, but it's also the way he treats you," he admitted. "But I know it's none of my business. I figure it's safer to keep my mouth shut all the way around."

"Kenny treats me the way he's always treated me," she responded, looking perplexed.

Didn't she see the way Kenny patronized her? Manipulated her? She gave in to his ridiculous whims far too easily. Just this morning, Kenny had insisted that the hotel needed a television for the living room, as if people came here to watch TV. And Bonnie had acquiesced, though Spencer knew for a fact that she despised television. Why didn't she stand up for herself?

"Really, it's none of my business," he finished lamely. "I'm just an employee around here."

"C'mon, Spencer, don't give me that. You're more than my employee and you know it."

He met her statement with a wary look. "No, I didn't know that. In fact, I distinctly remember you putting me firmly in my place as an employee...and nothing more."

Bonnie maneuvered herself inside the cab, then bent her head forward as she turned the ignition key. Her face was hidden by the curtain of her wavy blond hair. "I never meant to rule out friendship."

Friendship. The words seemed a pale ghost compared with what Spencer knew was possible between them.

Bonnie raised her voice slightly to be heard over the roar of the truck's engine. "Anyway, I said some things to you that night I didn't mean—or at the least, I said them in a way that wasn't very nice." Her words rushed out. "I have a tendency to overreact, especially when someone catches me off guard."

He was surprised at her admission. "I'm not defending my actions," he found himself saying, "but was my suggestion so unexpected?"

"Maybe not." She took a deep breath. "I was more surprised at myself than you." With that she threw the truck into reverse and backed quickly out of the carport, gravel flying, before Spencer could respond.

"Well, *damn*!" he said aloud as he ambled back up the driveway. Her own abandoned response to his kisses had surprised her, and that's why she'd pulled back. Was that what she meant? She'd certainly given him something to think about while she was in Little Rock.

He'd scarcely closed the front door behind him when Kenny's strident voice boomed at him from across the lobby. "Is she gone?"

Spencer nodded, watching the other man suspiciously.

Ken clapped his hands together gleefully, then picked up the phone at the front desk. As he dialed, Marmalade awoke from his nap, awarded Ken a disdainful hiss and stalked away, his fluffy tail waving like a red flag.

Spencer was overcome with curiosity about this phone call as he headed up the stairs to resume his chores. What was the twerp up to now?

"Hello, Norm?" said Ken. "You can bring the truck up now... I don't think you'll have any problem fitting it in one load. There's one love seat, one rocking chair, one armchair, and the big camelback sofa from the living room."

Spencer gave up all pretense of sweeping and leaned over the balustrade to better hear the one-way conversation. Ken was getting rid of furniture. This was serious.

"And you'll have it back middle of next week?" Ken asked. "Great, see you when you get here."

Spencer sighed with relief. At least the furniture was coming back at some point.

A few minutes later a white panel truck pulled up in front of the inn. Spencer sauntered leisurely through the lobby just as two burly men, directed by Ken, picked up the love seat and hauled it out the front door.

"What's going on?" Spencer asked casually.

Ken turned to him and smiled that too-friendly smile. "I'm surprising Bonnie by having the furniture reupholstered. It's so worn—gives the inn a tacky image. And image is everything in the marketing game."

Spencer bit his tongue to keep from retorting. The fabric on the love seat might be a bit worn, but it was also the original period upholstery. "What are you having it covered with?" he asked cautiously.

"The sample's in on my desk. Go have a look, if you want." He dismissed Spencer with a wave of his hand.

His desk? Spencer thought as he headed for the cubbyhole under the stairs that served as an office. Until a few days ago that had been Bonnie's desk.

He spied the fabric sample as soon as he walked through the office door, and he gasped in horror. Ken had chosen a wild geometric print for the Victorian furnishings. Bonnie would be surprised, all right.

There was a note beside the fabric swatch with the name of the upholsterer, a phone number and an alarming dollar figure, a quote for the job, Spencer guessed.

When he reentered the lobby, Ken was standing at the front door, waving goodbye to the men who'd taken the furniture.

"Excuse me, Ken," he said in his most subservient tone, "but isn't that fabric pattern a little...modern for antiques?"

Ken smiled confidently. "Textiles are my business, Guthrie. I saw that type of fabric all over Paris. It's the latest, most chic thing."

"But for antiques?" Spencer persisted.

Ken's smile faded. "Listen, Guthrie, am I missing something? I mean, do you own part of the inn? Or are you the *housekeeper*?" He pronounced the final word as if it were synonymous with *scum*.

Spencer didn't dignify the question with an answer, but the muscles in his jaw tightened. He found himself measuring Ken up, pound for pound, wondering if he could take him. He looked down and discovered that his hands were balled into fists.

Good Lord, did this guy have him so far off balance that he'd stoop to brawling like a juvenile delinquent? He made an effort to relax and deal with this problem sensibly.

"I know you want to surprise Bonnie," he said. "But if she comes back to find that geometric stuff on her furniture, she's going to pitch a fit."

"You let me worry about that," Ken replied, the smile returning. "I can handle Bonnie. Besides, it's my furniture, too. It's been in my family for more than a hundred years."

Spencer had never felt so powerless in his life. For the first time, he truly understood what it meant to hold a job with no power and no prestige. Briefly he reconsidered punching Ken right between his beady little eyes, then gave up the idea. Getting himself thrown in jail for assault wouldn't help save Bonnie's furniture.

He nodded and retreated to the kitchen, where, if he was lucky, he'd have some privacy.

What was the name of that doctor Bonnie was seeing in Little Rock? Brewer? No, Brewster. Picking up the wall phone receiver, he dialed Little Rock information. Soon he had the doctor's office on the line. He left a message for Bonnie to call him the moment she stepped through the door.

Spencer thought it couldn't get much worse. But an hour later he realized that this was only the beginning of Ken Chapman's reign of terror.

The chalkboard that sat unobtrusively on an easel by the stairway had caught his eye. This morning Bonnie had written the day's dinner special on it in her graceful, flowing script: fried catfish fillets, garden salad, corn bread, green beans and strawberry pie with ice cream, $6.95. Now that message was gone. In its place was another menu, written in Ken Chapman's bold, almost illegible printing: quiche lorraine, Waldorf salad or almond soup, steamed asparagus with hollandaise, strawberry tart, $10.95.

Was the man out of his mind? Ten dollars and ninety-five cents for quiche? At the very least, Ken had better be a good cook. There was no way on God's green earth that Spencer could produce that meal.

When the phone rang a few minutes later, Spencer dropped an arm load of towels and raced for the front desk, but Ken, who had just come through the door with two sacks of groceries, beat him to it.

Spencer hovered nearby, certain from the tone of Ken's voice that he was talking to Bonnie.

"Why, no, nothing's wrong," Ken said easily. "I can't imagine why he called...., Well, all right, I'll see if I can find him." Putting his hand over the mouthpiece, he turned swiftly toward Spencer, an accusing expression on his sharp features. "You say one word about the furniture, and so help me I'll fire you," he whispered.

"I'll take my chances," Spencer murmured as he took charge of the phone, knowing full well Ken would never carry out his threat, not with ten guests expected within the hour and several beds still to be made.

Bonnie waited at the other end of the line, wondering what in heaven's name was going on. When the receptionist at Dr. Brewster's office had given her the message, her first suspicion was that the hotel had burned down. Her second suspicion, a much more pleasant one, was that Spencer wanted to comment on that little tidbit she'd left him to ponder as she'd departed that morning. Realistically she deduced the actual reason for his call had little to do with her overactive imaginings.

She was right.

"Bonnie, Spencer. I've been looking all over for that little gizmo you use to slice hard-boiled eggs."

"You made a long-distance call to ask me that? Did you try the bottom left drawer by the dishwasher? Or just use—"

He halted her speech with a loud whisper. "Bonnie! That's not really why I called. I had to wait until Ken left the room."

"Oh?"

"I hate to be a stool pigeon...it's just that there's something going on here that, um, could have permanent, debilitating repercussions on—"

"Spencer, in English, please?"

"Ken's having all your furniture reupholstered in a red-yellow-and-blue corduroy geometric print," he blurted out. "I can't stop him."

"Oh, my heavens! That little sneak!" Bonnie clamped a hand over her mouth when she realized she had the attention of every occupant of the waiting room. "I already told him we didn't have room in the budget for redecorating."

"Some guy named Norm took the furniture away a couple of hours ago. I've got his number," Spencer offered.

"Oh, good. I know Norm. He's so slow he probably wouldn't even start the job till next month, so there's no danger I can't stop him in time."

Spencer gave her the number.

"Don't say anything to Ken," she cautioned. "I'll take care of it. Anything else?"

"Well...I thought I was going to miss you this weekend. Now I'm sure of it."

That brought a wash of heat to Bonnie's face. "I'll, um, miss you, too," she mumbled quickly. Then, in a more normal voice, "Just do your best with Kenny. You have my permission to take the necessary measures to keep him in line."

"Can I lock him in the cellar?"

"Spencer!"

"So give us a report on Fireman's Training School," Spencer asked Jenny that afternoon as the small group of graduate students settled onto the grass, in the shade of a big oak in the Student Center courtyard.

"It's not too bad," Jenny said, doodling nervously on the cover of a notebook. "Now that the guys can see that I work just as hard as they do, they're coming to accept me. And to tell you the truth—" she paused dramatically "—I think I may actually become a fire fighter."

The rest of the class whistled and cheered, Spencer included. He'd been surprised and pleased when Jenny had actually pursued enrollment in the training school. She'd gone much further than the actual class assignment required.

"What about you, Dr. Guthrie?" Randy asked. "How's the maid business? Are you having any luck with that jerk of a new boss?"

"I never said Ken was a jerk," Spencer said.

"He sounds like one," said Celia Fredericks in her frankly outspoken way.

"Whatever. No, I'm not having any luck convincing him to treat his hired help like human beings. He's as impossible to work for as ever. Now what about you, Randy? Did you apply for the receptionist's job?"

"I, um..." Randy stared up at the umbrella of oak leaves above them. "No. But I did work on my résumé."

"You have to actually apply for the job before you can complete the assignment," Spencer reminded him, though he was sure Randy was fully aware of that fact. He was otherwise an excellent student, and Spencer didn't want to fail him, but the personal experience gained through the employment assignment was an essential requirement for passing the course. Spencer believed that now more than ever.

"We want to hear more about the Sweetwater Inn," Jenny said, breaking the uncomfortable silence. "You haven't told us any good stories this week."

"I'm fresh out of good stories," Spencer said. For some reason, discussing his role at the inn with his students had become uncomfortable for him. What had started out as a simple exercise had turned into something altogether too personal to be discussed with a bunch of kids.

"Has the Southern belle learned anything about discrimination?" Celia asked.

"She's not a Southern belle," Spencer retorted hotly. "I was wrong to call her that. It just goes to show you that none of us are immune to harboring incorrect preconceived notions."

His students stared at him as if he'd grown another head.

Chapter Five

Bonnie did manage to extract some enjoyment out of her weekend in Little Rock. Dr. Brewster liberated her from her crutches by outfitting her with a walking cast, and she found the comparative freedom a vast improvement. She spent hours riding around the mall in her motorized cart, trying on anything that met her fancy, ruling out only those items that were outrageously expensive. She went wild in the intimate apparel store, filling her shopping bag with panties and camisoles and teddies and nightgowns made of the most luxurious, almost decadent fabrics and laces.

Several times she caught herself examining some silky scrap of a garment, envisioning herself in it—sans the cumbersome cast, of course—with Spencer looking on. The spontaneous fantasy made her blush furiously and wonder where her sanity had gone, but nonetheless his imaginary smile of approval kept convincing her to add to her purchases. She believed it to be a harmless mental exercise. But when she got back to the hotel room and examined what she'd bought, she was astounded at her own extravagance.

The new clothes had been long overdue, she reminded herself. She made up for going over her budget by eating at the local fast-food emporium instead of a pricier restaurant.

By the time she was headed back to Royal Springs early Monday morning, she felt refreshed and optimistic. Twice Spencer had called her at her hotel to check on her welfare. Their conversations were brief, but his concern pleased her to no end. He hadn't mentioned any further catastrophes concerning the inn, although a slight edge in his voice made her suspect that he wasn't telling her everything.

She thought again about the upholstery incident and was not quite as angry as she had been. A quick phone call to Norm had convinced him to put the job on hold, and that gave her some time to figure out a more permanent solution to the problem. But what if this problem was only a symptom of an even bigger problem?

"So, Kenny, we're stretching our wings, are we?" she queried aloud. But after all, he did have a lot of lost time to make up for. She felt certain that when he realized she was willing to compromise and share decisions, he'd stop trying to exert his authority so strenuously. And meanwhile she'd simply have to deal with whatever he dished up.

She came through the front door of the inn, her arms filled with boxes and shopping bags, fully expecting someone, preferably Spencer, to jump to her assistance. She looked forward to seeing him again more than she liked to admit. But no one greeted her.

She set down her packages by the door and looked around to see what was what. Then she gasped.

The lobby looked bare without its usual furnishings. Someone had dragged a couple of small chairs in from the living room in an attempt to fill space, resulting in a sparse, needy effect. But that wasn't what shocked Bonnie. What she found disturbing were the four men on ladders who were gingerly lowering the lobby's crystal chandelier.

She clumped across the polished wood floor, full of outraged purpose. On her way she caught sight of the chalkboard menu. *Hearts of palm? Crab tortellini?* One disaster at a time. She'd deal with that later.

When she was almost directly under the shimmering, fragile light fixture, she finally spoke to the workmen—softly, so as not to startle anyone.

"Excuse me, but what are you doing?"

"Oh, it's you, Bonnie." It was the voice of Floyd Ingram, the local electrician. "Kenny asked me to replace this here light. There're so many crystals missing, you see, and he says he can't find replacements. He's got a new fixture on order. Course, it won't be here till next week some time, but I've got an anxious buyer for this one, and Kenny said it'd be okay if I—"

"Wait, stop!" Bonnie had to do something to halt Floyd's endless explanation, or they'd be standing there all day. "It's not okay. Colonel Chapman brought this chandelier here from Alabama. This fixture predates the Civil War. The crystals were imported from Austria. And you'll take it out of here over my dead body," she said, with more ferocity than she knew she had in her.

Floyd looked contrite. "Sorry, Bonnie. I just naturally assumed you approved, though I must say I was

surprised." He turned his attention toward his helpers.
"Okay, boys, let's bolt it back up where it was."

Bonnie was a bit surprised herself that her wishes had
been honored so immediately over Kenny's. Then again,
the locals like Floyd Ingram, and Norm, for that matter,
knew her in a way they didn't know her brother-in-law.
While Kenny had been running wild all over the county,
she'd been baby-sitting for Floyd's kids. And while
Kenny had been doing Lord knows what in Europe's hot
spots, Bonnie had been here, sharing the vagaries of the
local economy with Floyd and Norm and other small-
business owners like herself. She'd been a faithful cus-
tomer, and her checks were always good.

"What should we tell Kenny?" Floyd asked her.

"Tell him—" she started, then stopped. If she went
head to head with Kenny she'd only make matters worse.
"Don't tell him anything. I'll take care of it."

Her brain was working fast and furious as she watched
the workmen put the bolts back into place. She knew
where to get replacement crystals. She hadn't bought
them before, because they were so frightfully expensive.
But if she ordered them right away, Kenny wouldn't have
any excuse for a new chandelier.

"Ah, Mr. Ingram?" she asked as the men gathered
their things to leave.

"Yes, ma'am?"

"Just out of curiosity, were we coming out ahead, or
behind, with this little chandelier exchange?"

"You were going to come out ahead—by quite a bit, as
a matter of fact. But the new light sure isn't as pretty as
the old one."

Bonnie was pondering this information as she made
her way into the dining room toward the kitchen. She felt
suddenly alone and afraid, for herself and for the inn.

Kenny was doing more than stretching his wings; he was in full flight and he seemed to be headed for some destination beyond her imagination.

She decided to find Spencer. Surely he would know what to do.

"Miss Bonnie?" It was Theo who found her first, however. He leaned his head through the swinging door from the kitchen just as she started to enter. His smile broadened when his eyes met hers. "I thought I heard your voice. I declare, I've never been so glad to see you." He came forward and put a companionable arm around her shoulders, squeezing tightly.

"I've only been gone a couple of days," she said, surprised at the gesture. Though Theo was unfailingly kind, he was not normally demonstrative.

"A lot can happen in a couple of days." He looked over his shoulder, as if he expected someone to be eavesdropping.

"You mean about the furniture, the chandelier—and the menu?" she asked, remembering the chalkboard.

"That, and some other stuff."

There was more? Oh, heavens.

"I see you're walking again, after a fashion," Theo observed. "Can you wander out to the garden with me? We can have a chat there, in private."

Bonnie's ankle wasn't bothering her in the least, so she made the short trek out to the garden, both eager and afraid to hear what else had gone on in her absence.

Reminded by a growling stomach that she hadn't had breakfast, she snatched a ripe, sun-warmed plum from a tree on her way out to the garden. She sat on the grass to munch on the fruit, hoping it would calm her sudden queasiness.

Theo picked up a bushel basket and began the task of locating all the ripe tomatoes and other vegetables. "To start with," he began, stooping to peek under the leaves of a squash plant, "I don't know why I'm bothering to pick any vegetables. Kenny refuses to use most of them, says they're too common for his new menus. So he goes to the gourmet store two counties away to buy endive, and some kind of ruffly lettuce, and hearts of palm, and scallions. They're the same dad gum wild onions I pick out in the woods for free, but mine aren't good enough. And you know that beautiful string of catfish I caught Friday morning? He wouldn't use them. Spencer and me ended up having 'em for lunch yesterday, and what we didn't eat I had to freeze."

"Who's cooking these fancy meals?" she asked. "Where are the recipes coming from?" She was quite sure nothing like crab tortellini could be found in any of her recipe boxes.

"Spencer's doing the cooking—or trying to. Kenny has a cookbook he brought back from France with the recipes, but I think something gets lost in the translation. The food's not to my taste, anyway."

"What do the guests think?"

"The few who stick around for dinner haven't come back for seconds. Most of 'em head over to Little Bob's for barbecue. The food's a sight heartier and a whole lot cheaper."

Bonnie leaned back onto the warm grass and sighed. This was worse, much worse, than she'd anticipated. "What's Spencer think of all this?" she asked, staring up at the fleecy white clouds and wondering why Spencer hadn't mentioned these problems.

"Now that's kinda hard to tell. He's been awful quiet lately. But I gotta give him credit for being a patient son-of-a-gun. If I were him, I'd have walked outta here days ago and never looked back.''

At those words she sat up abruptly. ''Where is Spencer, anyway?'' She had to see him, talk to him. If he quit she'd be devastated. She couldn't have explained why, but the thought of losing Spencer right now, on top of her problems with Kenny, was just too miserable a prospect to consider.

''I imagine you'll find him in the cellar. A hot-water pipe broke early this morning, and Kenny wouldn't call the plumber. Said it was too expensive. So Spencer's been working on the repair.''

''And meanwhile our guests are without hot water? And no one's minding the front desk?''

''Yup.''

Bonnie wanted to cry with frustration. Kenny would spend hundreds of dollars on unnecessary reupholstering, yet he couldn't fork over a few measly bucks for a plumber. A case of misplaced priorities if she ever saw one. But crying wouldn't solve anything. Instead she took several deep breaths until the threat of tears passed, then stood decisively. Spencer would know what to do.

Finding Spencer wasn't difficult. All she had to do was follow the curses and clangs down the cellar stairs. He was working at an octopuslike conglomeration of pipes near the water heater, and he seemed to be intent on beating one of the tentacles to death.

He turned abruptly at the sound of her steps, brandishing the wrench. ''If you think you can do better—'' He cut himself off when he recognized her. His angry scowl was replaced with a welcoming smile. ''Oh, it's you. I thought it was Ken again, coming to tell me how I'm doing this all wrong.''

Bonnie couldn't respond for a moment. She was too intent on taking in the sight of him, shirtless and appealingly disheveled. Perspiration gleamed on every inch of his exposed skin; the added dampness had caused his hair to curl around the edges. She resisted the urge to pick up a towel from the nearby laundry basket to blot him dry.

When she realized she'd remained silent for a ridiculous amount of time, she blurted out the first inane thing that came to mind. "Aren't you hot?"

"Yeah, under the collar—if I had a collar," Spencer muttered, suddenly acutely aware of his state of undress. "I've been at this for hours on end, I've made four trips to the hardware store, and damn it—"

Bonnie took the wrench out of his hand, and set it aside. "Come on, don't waste any more energy on this. Let's go upstairs and call the plumber. We have bigger things to worry about than leaky pipes."

Spencer hastily pulled his T-shirt over his head, then followed her up the stairs, feeling silly for letting his temper get the best of him. Kenny had been needling him all weekend about this and that, and in the interest of preserving the peace Spencer had kept his mounting frustration in check. Pounding and cursing at these pipes had been a way to release that pent-up anger, but he hadn't intended for Bonnie to witness his lack of composure.

Bonnie. God, but she was a welcome sight. He hadn't been kidding when he'd told her he missed her. As she climbed the stairs ahead of him, one awkward step at a time, he catalogued her figure from this new angle. He liked the curve of her shoulder blades under her light cotton sweater, and the way her denim skirt hugged her hips before flaring out to swirl around her calves.

"Hey, you're walking!" he noted, smiling broadly.

"It's more like clumping, actually. But I feel like a new person without those blasted crutches."

"And you did something to your hair."

"Just a trim. I'm surprised you noticed."

He noticed everything about her, from the department-store scent of her new clothes to the color of the polish on her bare toenails. Yet she still seemed oblivious of the effect her nearness had on him.

They emerged from the dim cellar into the lobby. Spencer blinked several times to adjust to the bright light.

"Did you know about the chandelier?" Bonnie asked suddenly.

"You mean about how it dates back to before the Civil—"

"No, I mean about Kenny's plans for getting rid of it."

"You've got to be kidding."

"Wish I was. I returned this morning just in the nick of time to prevent Floyd Ingram from carrying it out the front door." Then she added, more to herself than Spencer. "No wonder Kenny insisted you fix the pipes yourself. He didn't want you to catch him selling the chandelier."

Spencer was horrified at Ken's new level of audacity. "What did he plan to do, leave a gaping hole in the ceiling?"

"No, he wanted to replace it with a less valuable fixture and make a profit on the exchange. Maybe he thought he could use the profit to pay for the reupholstering. That makes some sense, I suppose. I just never suspected Kenny could cause so much trouble in so little time."

Spencer, on the other hand, had a sneaking suspicion that their troubles were only starting. Something about Ken's methods, aside from their sheer sneakiness, didn't sit quite right. If Ken honestly believed he was doing what was best for the hotel, why was he being so underhanded?

Much to Spencer's discomfort, Ken was just coming through the front door as he and Bonnie were entering the office.

"Well, welcome back, Bonnie Sue," he greeted cheerily, plopping two bags of groceries on the front desk. Marmalade took one look at who was invading his space and sped away in an orange streak, not even bothering to hiss at Ken this time.

Ken looked pointedly at Spencer. "Plumbing done?"

"Just about," Bonnie said, rushing the words out before Spencer had a chance to reply. "Need some help putting away the groceries?"

"No, no, I can take care of it," Ken answered, unobtrusively standing between Bonnie and the brown bags stamped in red with "Le Gourmet Shoppe." Then he eyed Spencer critically. "If you're done with the plumbing, get cleaned up. We've got some prep work to do for dinner." With that, he took charge of his groceries and turned to leave. He paused for a moment to stare up at the chandelier, as if wondering why it was still there. Spencer thought Ken might say something, but in the end he simply shook his head and walked on toward the kitchen.

"Prep work?" Bonnie asked as they went into the office.

Spencer was still struggling to subdue the urge to relieve Ken of a few of his teeth. That urge was coming more and more often these days. "I imagine he wants me to stuff tortellini. That's what's on the menu tonight. I had no idea when I took this job that I'd be getting French and Italian cooking lessons in the bargain."

Abruptly Bonnie pulled him into the small office, which seemed suddenly even smaller, and shut the door. "I had no idea, either, Spencer. I'm sorry it's turned out this way. But please, please don't quit. I can do some of the cooking, if that would help."

Quit? Leave Bonnie at the mercy of the devious Ken? The thought had never entered his mind. "I'm not going anywhere," he reassured her, laying both of his hands on her shoulders. She felt so frail and vulnerable. All Spencer could think about right then was protecting her from the evils of the world, and that included the unscrupulous Ken Chapman.

But who would protect her from Spencer Guthrie? a small, internal voice asked as his thoughts wandered of their own accord from protection to seduction. God, did she have any idea how desirable she was when she looked so lost and scared? What would she do, right now, if he just lowered his head a few inches and touched her sweet, inviting lips with his own? Even as the thought formed he moved in closer.

Her eyes held his, unflinching but also unreadable.

At the last moment he straightened his arms and pulled himself back. What the hell did he think he was doing? He'd never in his life taken advantage of a woman in a vulnerable position, and he wasn't about to start now. What Bonnie needed was help and advice, not seduction.

Now isn't the time, Bonnie. He pleaded silently with his eyes before turning his back toward her. It was only when she was out of his line of vision that he was able to talk aloud.

"Why did you tell Ken I was almost done with the plumbing?"

There was a pause before Bonnie answered. He could hear the strain in her voice. "What he doesn't know won't hurt him."

"But he'll find out eventually, won't he? Next time he looks at the checkbook."

"Fine. I'll deal with it, then."

"That's the spirit."

He turned back to face her then, relieved to see she was smiling. The tension between them dissolved quickly.

Bonnie sat down at the desk and picked up the phone to call for the plumber. "There's something to be said for postponing unpleasantness.... Hello, Ned? Bonnie Chapman. I have a hot-water pipe that needs fixing." She quickly hammered out the details, then hung up. "He'll be here and gone before Kenny knows the difference."

"And what will you do about the chandelier?" Spencer asked.

"That's an easy one." She fished around in the desk drawer for a business card, then picked up the phone once again. Within the span of a minute or two she'd placed an order for some new crystals to replace the ones missing from the old chandelier. "Now when Ken asks me why I sent Floyd away, I'll explain that the new crystals are on order so there's no need for a whole new fixture. He can hardly argue with that logic."

Spencer wrinkled his brow in thought as he studied her self-satisfied expression. "You're being just as sneaky as him, you know."

She took umbrage at that. "I prefer to think of it as being creative, maybe even clever. I'm fighting sneakiness with cleverness...." When she saw the dubious expression on his face, however, she abandoned that line of logic. "All right, I'm being sneaky," she admitted. "But he's driving me to it."

"There is a better way to handle this, you know."

"Spencer, we can't lock him in the cellar."

"No, I'm serious this time. The man does have to be put in his place—but figuratively speaking."

Bonnie couldn't disguise the elation she felt. Spencer was going to help her! "What do you mean to do?" she asked.

"Whoa, wait a minute. I never said *I'd* be the one to do it."

"Why not? You always know exactly what to say. You could reason with him, man to man."

"I may be a man," Spencer agreed, "but I happen to be just a lowly housekeeper. You're the logical one to confront him. You are half owner of this hotel, and you have the right to veto some of his ideas."

"He'd never listen to me," she said, exasperated, her newfound hope melting away like a sugar cube in the rain.

"Bonnie, I'd love to help, really. But in case you hadn't noticed, I'm not the knight-in-shining-armor type. Rescuing damsels in distress is way out of my league. Besides, there's no call to rescue someone who's perfectly equipped to rescue herself."

"I can't do this by myself," Bonnie argued. "I've tried to talk sense to him before. I tried to go over the books with him. I tried to explain how the budget is set up, but he just ignores it. He has his own philosophy about how the inn can become the trendiest, most luxurious hotel in all of Arkansas, and apparently he's going full speed ahead with his plans, regardless of how I feel."

"He has no right to do that," Spencer argued.

"But maybe he does," Bonnie countered after a few moments' pause, her fingertips tapping the desktop as she spoke. "After all, the Sweetwater Inn is Kenny's ancestral home. It's been in his family for generations. If anyone is a usurper, it's me."

"You were Sammy Chapman's wife," Spencer said softly. The mention of Bonnie's husband still made him slightly uncomfortable. "It was his choice to leave you his half of the inn. Don't you feel you should run the place the same way he would have?"

She sighed. "I had my chance to run things. I haven't been wildly successful. Maybe it's time to let someone else have a try at it."

"But you *have* been successful," he said. "You're operating in the black."

"But maybe Kenny can do better. Maybe his ideas will work, if we just give them time."

"That's a royal cop-out, if you'll excuse the sixties terminology. You're rationalizing your way out of standing up to him. And while you're waiting to get your courage up, the inn might go under."

"No." Bonnie shook her head vehemently. "Before that happens, I'm sure Kenny and I will find a way to work out responsibilities between us. We're still in an adjustment period. It'll just take a little more time."

Spencer started to offer further objections, then stopped himself. If she didn't want to assert her rights, who was he to tell her what to do? No matter what he said, she still wanted *him* to do something; in fact her eyes were silently pleading for him to rescue her.

He couldn't fight her battles for her. That would go too much against his grain. Anyway, Bonnie wasn't really a damsel in distress, although at the moment she probably felt like one. She had more innate intelligence and fortitude than just about any person he knew, and that was all she needed to confront her brother-in-law and preserve her status as an owner of this hotel.

Her problem, he decided, was that Kenny intimidated her. That was something he couldn't help her with until she made up her mind to stand up to him. Who could tell when that might be?

"Well, Bonnie," he said, standing to go, "it's your hotel. As an employee I'll cooperate with Kenny, if that's what you want me to do. But if you change your mind about confronting him . . ." He left it at that.

Bonnie stared at the door long after he'd left. Why had she thought Spencer could solve all her problems? she wondered. What had she expected him to do, make Kenny disappear? He had no more influence over Kenny than she did, even if he was a large, strong and very forceful man. He could probably beat Kenny to a pulp in a physical confrontation, but barring that, he didn't have much to hang over Kenny's head.

Face it, girl, Kenny is your relative and your problem and no one else's.

Her mind drifted back to something only slightly less disturbing but infinitely more intriguing—the moment when Spencer had almost kissed her. What had made him pull back, she wondered? If ever she'd issued a silent invitation, that was it. Why hadn't he listened?

Her body tingled again at the memory of his nearness. She was glad when the sound of the bell at the front desk interrupted her reverie; otherwise, she might well have sat there the rest of the day, lost in pleasant but pointless fantasy instead of facing up to reality.

When she emerged from the office, she found four young women standing expectantly before the desk, their arms loaded with books and folders.

"Hi, I'm Bonnie Chapman. Can I help you?" she asked, briskly pulling the registration book from under the desk.

The obvious leader of the group stepped forward. "We'd like two rooms for the night, adjoining if possible. We have a big sociology test to study for, and it's just too noisy in the dorm."

"Distracting," another girl added.

"You've come to the right place," Bonnie said as she indicated where they should sign in. "Around here it's quiet as a church, at least for the moment. I'll put you in Rooms 204 and 205—oh, but I better check and see if they're made up. If you'll just have a seat—" She gestured toward the sparse lobby furnishings before beginning her ascent up the stairs.

"Excuse me?"

Bonnie paused and looked over her shoulder. "Yes?"

"Don't you have a housekeeper to make up the rooms?" The young woman who'd posed the question was trying awfully hard not to laugh.

"I do, as a matter of fact," Bonnie answered, putting two and two together. These were some of Spencer's classmates, who'd come to check up on him. "But he's busy with something else at the moment." She continued up the stairs, though she was curious to know what these cheeky little coeds thought of Spencer. Did he date any of them? A sudden stab of jealousy, though totally inappropriate, prevented her from pursuing that line of speculation.

To her relief, she found that the rooms were in tip-top shape. She hurried back downstairs, as fast as the cast would allow her to hurry, to find that Theo had magically appeared to help with the small bags the girls had brought with them. She gave him what she hoped was a reassuring smile as he escorted the giggling group to their rooms.

The prettiest of the young women, with a cloud of black hair and huge almond-shaped eyes, paused on the staircase behind the others and addressed Bonnie. "Spencer Guthrie does work here, doesn't he?"

"Yes," Bonnie answered cautiously.

"That's what I'd heard." The girl batted her long lashes a couple of times before following the others.

Poor Spencer, Bonnie thought. There were so many young, unattached women in a college setting, and they'd naturally be attracted to someone as mature and good-looking as Spencer. He must constantly have to fend them off. Then again, maybe he didn't mind the inconvenience. That thought hardly gave her any comfort.

Spencer cursed the broken pipe once more as he endured an icy shower. He washed up in record time, though not out of any sincere desire to hurry on to his next task. He wasn't sure if he could withstand another session of Ken orally translating a recipe, then criticizing step-by-step as Spencer tried to follow directions.

How would Kenny look wearing tortellini? Spencer wondered, smiling as he pictured it in his mind. He wouldn't resort to that kind of tactic, though, no matter how tempted he was. He'd promised Bonnie that he'd cooperate, and that meant he'd do his level best to prevent Ken from firing him.

That made him wonder. If Ken did try to fire him, would Bonnie fight to keep him? He sighed, wishing he could believe that she would.

By the time dinner was ready that night, Spencer had to admit that it was one of his better efforts. The crab recipe had thankfully come out of an American gourmet cooking magazine, so Ken was able to leave him alone to prepare it. It didn't taste half-bad, and by dressing it up with some fresh parsley and black olives the plates were attractive.

Not that he would have expected any of the hotel's guests to pay the outrageous price Ken had set, even if he'd been serving steak and lobster. So he was surprised when he peeked into the dining room and saw half a dozen people, chatting amiably with Bonnie as they sipped iced tea and waited for Spencer to serve them.

"I hope you have enough for four extra," Bonnie whispered to him as she stood to help him with the plates he'd brought out. "I forgot to tell you about the ladies in 204 and 205. They'll be down in just a few minutes."

"What ladies?" Spencer had thought the people sitting in the dining room represented all the guests they had at the moment.

"I checked them in a little earlier. Some students, studying for a test. A sociology test," she added.

Uh-oh, he thought as the hairs on the back of his neck stood at attention. *Trouble.*

"Do you need some help carrying out the rest of the plates?" she asked.

"I have it under control. Why don't you just relax and enjoy your dinner for once?" he scolded mildly, nudging her back into her chair. "You've been on your feet all day."

"But my toes aren't purple," she objected, starting to get up again.

Spencer gently pushed down on her shoulders. "There's no need for you to knock yourself.out. All the work's done. Now let me serve you."

She smiled and gave a sigh of resignation. "If you insist."

He started to smile back, but his facial muscles froze as soon as he saw who was headed across the lobby toward the dining room. Four of them. Four of his students, their faces plastered with nasty little conspiratorial smiles, just waiting for a chance to do their worst.

Why did students get such a kick out of tormenting a teacher? Was it because this was their one chance to have him at their mercy, instead of the other way around? From a psychological standpoint, it made sense, and the test he'd scheduled for tomorrow had probably filled them full of resentment. That didn't make it any easier for him to endure their pranks.

He wished he could threaten them with their grades, but that would hardly be ethical. Then another possibility came to him. Yes, that might do it. If he made a casual observation, that certainly wouldn't be compromising his ethics. And it just might work.

Quickly he served the other guests, as well as Bonnie, saving the tableful of students for last.

"Hi, Spence," said Vicki Cameron in an unusually familiar manner as he set a plate of pasta before her. "Have you, um, studied for the test? I bet the prof is going to stick it to us good this time."

At least she remembered not to blow my cover, Spencer thought, his relief tinged with guilt over his continued deception.

"Oh, I'm sure it won't be any harder, or easier, than his other tests," Spencer said carefully as he served the remainder of the dinners. "You know how it is with essay tests. Your grade depends a lot on just what mood the prof's in when he's doing the grading."

"What?" said Vicki, her dark head swiveling up to look at him.

"You know. If the prof's in a great mood, if he's had an easy week, he's apt to give higher grades. On the other hand, if he's feeling, say, overworked, the grades might come out lower, on the average. You know, I read once where they did this study of college professors..." But the students were no longer listening. They were eyeing each other, uncertainty plain in their questioning looks.

He headed back to the kitchen to get the iced tea pitcher for refills, confident that he'd taken care of at least one problem.

If only his other dilemma could be taken care of so easily. The memory of his conversation with Bonnie that afternoon kept nibbling at his conscience. Though he was tempted, he knew it would be wrong to interfere in her power struggle with Ken. Spencer was convinced that Bonnie needed to solve the problem herself. In doing so she would come to realize how strong and capable she really was, and ultimately that had to be good for her.

He'd made a sensible, rational decision to remain uninvolved. Why did it feel so much like betrayal?

He'd let himself get emotionally involved with her, that's why. Involvement between employer and employee was never a good idea, but it was especially stupid in his situation. Not only had he started off his association with Bonnie by lying about his reasons for wanting this job, but now the situation at the inn had turned into a potentially explosive one.

The romantic sparks flying between himself and Bonnie might be just enough to set off the dynamite, and he surely didn't want to be responsible for that.

He'd tried it before and failed, but this time he meant to keep his distance from Bonnie Chapman.

Chapter Six

Bonnie sat on a wooden swing suspended between two massive oak trees behind the inn, trying to get the better of her temper. She'd managed to keep the peace all week by letting Kenny have his way, but her patience was growing paper thin.

Just a few minutes earlier, he'd finally confronted her about the chandelier. When she'd explained how the replacement crystals were on order, he'd treated her to a patronizing look of disapproval and a shake of his expertly barbered blond head.

"I wish you wouldn't try to thwart my every effort," he said sullenly as she'd attempted to slide past him out of the office. "You're too set in your ways, Bonnie. You've got to untie my hands so I can make some changes. They're long overdue."

"I'm not tying your hands," she'd argued. "You've pretty much had a free rein the past couple of weeks. And

just because I'd like to keep a family heirloom chandelier hardly means I'm set in my ways."

He took an exasperated breath. "What will it take to
prove to you, to all of you, that I know what I'm doing?
Everyone around here has been complaining about my
new menus, yet you saw the crowd we had at dinner last
night. Meat and potatoes are passé. Vacationers want to
eat trendier food."

Bonnie had nodded a cautious agreement, but now she
wondered if she shouldn't have told Kenny the real reason they'd attracted a crowd for Spencer's chicken picata: she'd surreptitiously changed the price on the
chalkboard menu from $10.95 to $5.95, then made sure
she totaled the bills herself.

"And wait till you see the new furniture," Kenny had
continued, his disapproving frown vanishing as he
warmed to the subject of his own supposed accomplish-
ments. "It's going to brighten up that lobby a hundred
percent."

Again she had nodded, wishing she could truly agree
with him. She had managed to keep the reupholstering
project on hold for a little longer by casually suggesting
to Norm that the inn didn't have enough money in the
bank to pay for the job. Norm conveniently stalled Kenny
without her even having to ask.

But there was only so much behind-the-scenes maneu-
vering she could do. Things just couldn't continue like
this. It was as if a black thundercloud hung over the inn,
heavy and oppressive, just waiting to explode into a rag-
ing storm.

Perhaps if Bonnie had something useful to do she
wouldn't feel so on edge, she reasoned. She was fast becoming an anachronism around the inn, a lumbering,
useless dinosaur, and the idleness was driving her crazy.

She had never experienced idleness before. From the time she was a very small child, she'd always had a million chores to do in order to help her mother keep their meager little household functioning. If she'd ever had an hour to herself to read a magazine or take a bubble bath, she'd considered it pure luxury.

Even during her brief marriage, she hadn't acted like any indolent lady of the manor. There were always meals to be prepared and laundry to be done, or a garden that needed weeding.

Now the inactivity was getting to her. Kenny had pretty much taken over her office and all the paperwork. Spencer had the cooking and housekeeping chores well in hand. For someone who two weeks ago had looked uncomfortable holding a broom, he'd adapted quite nicely. Even the garden seemed to be taking care of itself, and Theo could handle the few weeds that popped up.

When she'd been running the inn single-handedly, all she could think about was how burdensome the responsibility was, and how inadequate her efforts sometimes seemed. But now that she was idle, she realized something else: her work had been challenging and, in its way, rewarding. And maybe she hadn't been doing such an inadequate job, after all—not if she judged herself against Kenny.

She missed it. She missed running the inn.

Lifting the hair off the back of her neck, she let the gentle breeze cool the dampness there. Was she blowing her frustration out of proportion? Or had she made a disastrous decision in letting Kenny take over?

A cold spray of water fanned quickly across her, abruptly intruding on her musings. Reflexively she jumped up onto her good leg, shaking the water droplets off her loose cotton blouse and out of her hair.

"Spencer!" she called out when she realized he had deliberately doused her with the garden hose. "What do you think you're doing?" She was laughing, though, despite herself. The water had done little more than surprise her, and she was actually very pleased that Spencer was paying any personal attention to her at all. Lately he'd been so reserved and businesslike she was beginning to think she'd imagined that almost-kiss a few days ago.

"I think I'm washing the windows," he answered her, closing the nozzle and dropping the hose. "And I think I'm done." He came over to her and sat down on the other end of the swing. "As a matter of fact, by some miracle I've completed every item on the list Ken gave me this morning. So how about it? Do you think I merit a couple of hours off?"

Bonnie shrugged. "I have no objections."

"Would you care to join me? I had in mind a picnic in the woods."

She was so surprised by the invitation that she didn't speak for a moment. When she did, she was amazed that her voice came out sounding natural. "Sure, why not— as long as you don't plan on hiking too far afield. My ankle isn't bothering me much anymore, but I'm still not up to long-distance walking."

"If you get tired I'll carry you piggyback," he offered, his eyes twinkling with mischief.

This was the Spencer she remembered from their first couple of days together. She was so relieved to see that warm, teasing side of him that she didn't bother to think too closely about what the logistics of a piggyback ride would mean.

While Spencer went to wash his face and change clothes, Bonnie found a picnic basket in the basement.

She had to chase a few spiders out of it, but otherwise it was in good shape, though she knew it had been years since she'd been on an outing of this sort.

She packed it up with some of the leftover chicken picata, a hastily assembled salad of vegetables fresh from the garden, some croissants from that morning's breakfast, and two pieces of what Kenny insisted on calling strawberry tart, but which was actually just a plain old pie. Spencer had baked this one, even the crust. It was slightly thicker and lumpier than hers would have been, but definitely acceptable. His cooking abilities continued to surprise her. When the food supply was to her satisfaction, she added two cans of ginger ale, some paper plates and napkins, silverware and an old tablecloth.

She met Spencer on the back porch a few minutes later. How did he manage to look and smell so fresh, she wondered, when she herself was feeling decidedly wilted from the heat? She never saw him ironing clothes; neither had she seen him bringing home clothes from the dry cleaners. Yet his casual cotton shirt had crisp creases in the sleeves. Even his jeans looked pressed.

Another mystery about Spencer that didn't bear close scrutiny, she decided.

He took the picnic basket from her, then stooped partway down and held his arms away from his body. "Hop on."

"I can walk," she objected.

"You can walk," he agreed, then added, "about as efficiently as a one-legged cricket. Come on, let me give you a lift."

He was right, so she gave in and climbed onto his back. He lifted her, seemingly without effort, and she wrapped her arms around his neck. He felt good. Solid, reassuring...and sexy as all get-out. Her skin began to tingle from the outside in, until the sensation reached the center of her body. It was all she could do not to squirm against him.

Think about something else, she commanded herself. His hair. This was the first time she'd had the opportunity to study his hair up close. Sunlight gleamed off an occasional golden streak in the light brown waves, so that it looked more than ever like polished birch. She tested its softness against her cheek, finding the texture very agreeable. Giving in to impulse, she leaned her head companionably against his and propped her chin on his shoulder.

"Do you have a favorite picnic spot?" he asked as he situated the basket between his hands and started toward the woods at a brisk pace. "If so, navigate the way."

Quickly she ran through all the possible locations for a picnic. There was one spot that she, Kenny and Sammy used to enjoy in their youth, but she rejected it almost immediately. She and Spencer should have a place all their own, with none of her memories associated with it.

"Head up that hill and around the bent-over oak," she directed. "We'll meet up with the creek, and then follow it upstream a ways until we come to a likely spot. Maybe we can even go for a swim—" She stopped herself, recalling the last time they'd gotten into the water together. "Oh, of course I can't swim," she added quickly. "I forgot about this dumb cast. And we didn't bring any bathing suits, anyway."

"Hmm. An interesting dilemma."

There was no mistaking the suggestive note in his voice. Whatever was going on with him, his interest in her as a woman was still evident. That half pleased her and half scared her out of her wits. When he treated her impersonally, it made her want him with a bittersweet intensity that was maddening. Yet when he was attentive like this, she had to resist the urge to run and hide under the nearest rock. Did she or did she not want to kindle the spark that obviously flared between them?

Bonnie tried not to ask herself any more difficult questions as the path brought them slowly up one of the hills that stood guard over the inn. She took in the scenery, the lush green canopy overhead, the crunch of the leaves under Spencer's shoes, the chatter of playful chipmunks and the shy purple wildflowers that peeked out from the undergrowth.

She'd taken this beauty too much for granted lately. How lucky she was to have such breathtaking sights practically in her backyard, and how lucky she was to be sharing them right now with Spencer.

She knew that she must be a heavy burden for Spencer to carry, particularly with the cast on her leg, and the picnic basket wasn't light, either. But his pace never slowed as he followed the steadily uphill path along the bank of Silver Creek. He was hardly even winded when he paused at the top of a rise to rest.

"Which way now?" he asked.

"Mmm, that way." She pointed in a direction she was sure she'd never been before. "But aren't you getting tired?"

"As much as I bicycle up and down the mountain roads, it takes a lot to tire me out." Actually he should have been exhausted, he realized as he trudged on in the direction she'd indicated. But Bonnie seemed light and soft as a cloud, and the feel of her limbs twined about him was so invigorating he could have scaled every mountain in the Ozarks if only she'd remain pressed up against him like this.

At the top of the next rise, they came upon a view of the mountains so spectacular that they were forced to make this their final destination. He eased her to the ground. His arm moved quite naturally around her shoulders as together they enjoyed the view of gently rolling, forested hills that seemed to stretch forever into the distance, reaching for the flawless blue sky.

Though no words were exchanged, he felt a closeness stealing over them like a soft blanket. He'd half expected her to shut him out. Lord knows why she was giving him a second chance, after the way he'd treated her over the past few days and the distance he'd deliberately put between them.

Distance. Yes, that's exactly what he'd tried to accomplish, foolishly believing that if he forced himself to think of Bonnie in only professional terms, his urge to involve himself in her personal life would go away.

Once again, he'd failed.

In fact, the more he tried to pull away from her, the more potent his desire for her became. And her obvious confusion over his attitude only made him feel guilty. He had finally decided this morning that he'd stop fighting his feelings, puzzling though they were, and try to reestablish the closeness they'd had a taste of before everything got thrown out of whack.

This time, of course, he knew better than to make any too-forward propositions. If she wanted moonlight and flowers and poetry, she was out of luck. He simply didn't believe in that sort of superficial courtship. But there was no law that said he couldn't move more slowly with her.

She sighed expansively. "It's been ages since I've really taken a good look at the mountains," she said. "They're spectacular, don't you think? Then again," she continued, without waiting for his answer, "I guess they have mountains where you come from. Are these as nice as the ones in California?"

"I'm not sure," he answered honestly. "California mountains are different than these. Flashier, perhaps. But this..." He waved his arm to indicate the panoramic view. "The Ozarks are more satisfying in some ways. More peaceful." And I'm sharing them with you, he wanted to add, but he held back. He'd take things one step at a time.

"How long are you planning to stay here—in Arkansas, I mean?" she asked. "Do you plan to finish school here?"

He winced inwardly as he remembered for the first time in days the real reason he'd come to work at the inn. He was deceiving Bonnie about his identity. If things were to work out between them, he would have to come clean. But not here, not now, when they were just beginning to talk and laugh together again. He'd tell her later, maybe tonight.

"I haven't made any plans to leave," he answered. And that was true. In fact, just yesterday he'd agreed to teach two classes next semester, and possibly more the following spring. He liked it here, enough that he hadn't even contemplated returning to L.A.

"Good." She expelled a long breath. "I'm not looking forward to hiring another maid."

Spencer winced again. Another reminder of his duplicity. He'd intended on taking this job for six weeks only, but that was before he understood the situation here. He knew he couldn't work as a housekeeper forever, but under no circumstances would he leave the inn until he was sure Bonnie had everything under control. In fact, maybe he could even find his own replacement, to save her the trouble. But just now he couldn't imagine anyone replacing him. He couldn't imagine leaving the Sweetwater Inn at all.

When he brought himself back to the present, he discovered Bonnie digging into the picnic basket. "I just packed up some leftovers, whatever was handy," she was explaining as she unfolded a blue-flowered cloth.

He grabbed two corners of the cloth and helped her wrestle it to the ground against the playful breeze. Quickly she anchored one corner with the basket, then plopped down on another corner.

He joined her, smiling for no reason in particular.

They systematically devoured every edible morsel they'd brought, laughing and teasing in a manner so familiar it was as if they'd known each other for years. But when the scraps were packed away, Bonnie grew noticeably more serious. Spencer waited a while for her to tell him what was on her mind, but when she remained silent he finally asked her:

"What is it, Bonnie? You look like a thundercloud."

She smiled weakly at that. "I was just wondering about something, and I might as well say it aloud. Why the sudden urge to take me on a picnic? Why now, when for the past week you've been doing your best imitation of a poker-faced butler?"

"Umm, because you looked like you needed cheering up?"

Judging from the skeptical tilt of Bonnie's eyebrow, Spencer guessed his glib response didn't satisfy her. He didn't want to burden her with the grisly details of his internal struggle, but he owed her an explanation that was a little closer to the truth.

"I've been trying to resist you," he said, scooting across the cloth until he was mere inches away from her.

"But I've come to the conclusion that you're completely irresistible."

And she was. Seemingly without either of them moving, she was in his arms—almost as if she'd materialized there. Her lips met his with no trace of her previous shyness. He tried his best to maintain a gentle kiss, a respectful kiss, but there was no way he could, not when she was kissing him back with such abandon.

After a few moments, however, she gently pulled away from him and leaned back against the blue-flowered cloth, her breathing rapid, her gray-green eyes large and full of questions.

"Irresistible," he repeated under his breath as he reclined beside her, propping his head on one elbow. A strand of her blond hair trailed over one shoulder and across her breast. He traced the strand with his finger, delighting in the feel of her firm nipple through her thin cotton shirt. And all the while, he watched her face, following the changing expressions there.

He cupped her breast in his hand, and the sensations of warmth and softness against his palm engendered a tightness in his throat, a tenseness in the pit of his stomach. Was he moving too fast? He felt he'd lost all sense of judgment, as if this were the first time he'd been intimate with a woman. But when he studied her features, he saw no signs of reluctance or disapproval, only a tremulous smile.

She began her own tentative exploration with her hands, testing the smoothness of his freshly shaved chin, the curve of his ear, his neck, the hard muscles of his shoulder. Every place she touched was ignited with velvet fire. Spencer closed his eyes and allowed himself to tumble into a world of sensations that hinted of the staggering potential between them.

A foreign thought tried to intrude upon his dreamy world. What would happen when Bonnie found out he'd been deceiving her? Would she kiss him or touch him like this if she knew the truth? But he pushed the thought away. Time enough for true confessions later.

Bonnie watched him with languorous eyes, allowing a strange, quiet elation to wash over her. Something special was happening, something that went well beyond a simple kiss or a lingering touch. *He* was the irresistible one, with all those muscles and sinews and that smooth warm skin that begged for a woman's caress....

She let her gaze wander to the open collar of his shirt, the tuft of soft brown hair that peeked out just above the last button. Impulsively she raised up and placed her lips right at that spot, letting her tongue tease the hollow place at the base of his neck.

Spencer let loose a small groan of pleasure. He couldn't remember ever being kissed in that particular spot before; the effect was strangely erotic. He leaned back to give her access to any part of him she chose to kiss, and she obligingly began to sample him like a smorgasbord. Her kisses, fraught with all the softness of moonlight and summer breezes, wandered from his neck to his jaw to his ear and back again.

The tension inside him built unmercifully, but still he held himself in check, knowing that Bonnie had no inkling of how fully she'd aroused him. This was no practiced seduction. In fact, he got the distinct impression she was satisfying her own curiosity rather than trying to please him.

He could only guess at the pleasure they could share once they both let go. And they would—some day soon. Maybe not today, for there were too many questions and doubts hanging over their heads, but soon.

His hands slipped under her shirt to span her tiny waist, rubbing his palms against the softness of her back. He longed for a day when he could spend hours on end discovering every sensitive inch of her skin.

When her mouth found his again, he was on his back and she was reclining against him, their bodies touching from chest to knee. If this were any other woman, he'd believe she was giving him the okay to proceed full speed ahead. But not Bonnie. Not his sweet, sexy Bonnie, so knowing and yet so innocent in some ways. He wasn't quite sure how to deal with a woman of her ilk—not when it came to lovemaking.

When the clumsy cast picked that moment to misbehave and bump him square in the knee, it provided an unwanted but sorely needed distraction. With what little control Spencer had left, he groaned and gently pushed her away.

"If you keep this up, I won't be responsible for the consequences," he teased, trying to coax a smile from her.

She didn't give him one. Instead she lowered her lashes and sat up, adjusting her blouse over her heaving breasts. Then she straightened her hair, smoothing it behind her shoulders. When finally she looked at him, however, she was far from composed.

"I—I don't know what happened. I've never... I completely forgot myself," she concluded, averting her eyes once again.

She was priceless. He'd never known a woman who would apologize for making him feel such fantastic things. Never mind the frustration. He'd endure it.

"You have my permission to forget yourself any time," he said as he sat up and quickly kissed her forehead. "But you'll have to forgive me if I make a similar transgression every now and then." He stood up quickly, before he was overtaken by another urge to kiss her. "Come on, we'd better get back. Ken frowns on extended lunch hours."

It took Bonnie the better part of the day to get over the aftereffects of her picnic with Spencer. She more or less floated around the inn on a euphoric cloud, happy to assist Theo in draining one of the mineral bath pools for cleaning, and positively beaming as she helped Spencer with dinner preparations.

Occasionally she wondered what would have happened if Spencer hadn't stopped things when he did. Would she have objected if he'd started to undress her? Would she have regretted it afterward if they'd made love in that beautiful spot on the side of a mountain?

The answer was probably no, to both questions. She objected to casual sex. But such intimacy between herself and Spencer could never be casual, because they shared something more than mere physical attraction.

Then again, wasn't that the way people usually justified making love when they weren't married, or even committed? And what exactly did she and Spencer have in the way of a relationship? They'd never been on a date. He wasn't what she'd call a boyfriend, or—what was that more modern term? A significant other? He wasn't one of those. Yet she felt closer to him in some ways than she ever had to any man, even Sammy. That closeness just didn't have a name.

Happy with that conclusion, she decided on a bath before dinner instead of her usual lightning-fast shower. She propped her cast on the side of the claw-footed tub and reveled in the purely feminine indulgence of floral-scented bubbles.

When she was glowing pink and warm from her bath, she opened the closet and pulled out a topaz silk dress she'd splurged on in Little Rock but hadn't yet worn. Instead of leaving her hair loose as she almost always did, she twisted it into an elegant knot on the crown of her head. She didn't try to delude herself; she was spiffing up just for Spencer, and he was sure to know it. That thought sent a shiver of anticipation down her spine.

She slipped on one open-toed pump and was pleased to discover that the added height of the heel matched up with the cast on her other leg and allowed her to walk more gracefully. As a final touch, she took a tiny sample of expensive perfume she'd been given at a department store and dabbed a bit behind each ear.

By the time she came down for dinner she was still early. The French doors leading to the living room were open, and she thought she saw the shadow of movement, so she went to investigate. She found Bernie Hoffman from the decorating center, measuring the walls. What now?

"Oh, hi, Bonnie," he greeted her cheerfully. "I'm just about finished up in here. I'll have the figures for you and Kenny shortly."

"What figures?"

"For the wallpaper." He worked something out on a pocket calculator while she let that sink in. The current wallpaper was authentic 1920s deco, hardly faithful to the Victorian architecture, but beautiful in its own right.

"I assume Kenny picked out the pattern?"

"Oh, I thought you'd seen it. Here, I have a sample in here somewhere—" He fumbled around with a notebook, finally coming up with a scrap of wallpaper.

Bonnie felt her stomach wrench when she saw it. It was a 1950s revival pattern, overlapping kidney-shaped blobs in turquoise and pink.

"It's..." Words failed her. "But not for this room. I think the old paper is fine, don't you?"

"Well, it's a little faded, and there are some water stains up in that corner."

"Hmm. Maybe we do need a change in here," Bonnie acquiesced. "But not that pattern. I'll come into the shop later this week and...no, no, that's not what I mean. I'm afraid there's been a mix-up. This old paper will have to stay."

"But Kenny said—"

"He was wrong. I'm sorry you had to come out here for nothing, Bernie."

Bernie smiled good-naturedly. "I don't mind. It was on my way home."

She walked Bernie to the front door, keeping a tight rein on her anger until he was gone. Even then, she quietly returned to the living room and closed the door before she finally gave in to a most undignified urge to beat her fist against something. Since Kenny's face wasn't handy, the top of a cherry wood table had to do.

Bang! The knickknacks on the table vibrated with her fury.

If she'd suspected it before, now she knew it beyond the shadow of a doubt: Kenny's judgment was awful. The worst! He didn't have the slightest idea what he was doing. Fifties wallpaper? In a Victorian hotel? *She* knew better than that.

If only she'd believed more strongly in her own judgment, Kenny's confidence and enthusiasm wouldn't have fooled her. As a shy girl she'd allowed him to do the same thing. She could remember trailing after him years ago and letting him lure her into his various projects, most of which ended in disaster—like the time he tried to build a raft from the rotting planks of an old dock and they'd nearly drowned themselves. Then there was the time he convinced her to jump off the roof using a homemade parachute.

While she no longer idolized Kenny as she had in those days, the patterns they had established as children were still very much a part of the way they dealt with each other now.

She clapped her hands together decisively. No more of that. Kenny would never willingly share responsibilities and decisions with her. And if she didn't do something to regain the ground she'd lost, she could well lose the inn. At the very least, she'd have to live with some horrid decorating sin for the rest of her life.

"Spencer's been right all along," she murmured aloud. She'd have to confront Kenny. She'd have to put her foot down and stop all this nonsense. But how did she do that? What was the first step?

She opened the living room doors and stepped out into the lobby. "Kenny!" she called out, heedless of who might be around to hear her bellowing. "Kenny Chapman, I want to speak to you!"

Spencer burst through the swinging kitchen door and trotted through the still-empty dining room, clutching a mixing bowl and whisk. He set them down on a table. "What is it? What's wrong?"

Just then Theo came through the front door. "I heard somebody hollering," he said, mopping the sweat from his brow with a bright yellow handkerchief. "Where's the fire?"

Bonnie felt herself redden with embarrassment. She hadn't meant to get the whole inn up in arms. "It's

Kenny," she answered in a much lower voice. "Nothing important. I'm just going to kill him, that's all."

Spencer and Theo exchanged puzzled looks. "What's he done this time?" Spencer finally asked. "Incidentally, he's out for the evening. Hot date."

Bonnie began to pace. Part of her was relieved that the confrontation would be postponed, but in a way she wanted to get it over with. "It's not important," she repeated. "I'll deal with it."

Spencer threw her a skeptical look.

"No, really. This time I won't sneak around behind his back. I'll confront him directly. I'll say, 'Kenny, you cannot change the wallpaper in the living room.' Period."

"Atta girl, Miss Bonnie!" Theo said. "You give what-for to that insolent pup." He gave her shoulder an encouraging squeeze before wandering off, muttering, "What for does he want to change the wallpaper?"

Spencer's initial reaction, however, was a bit more cautious. "Are you sure, Bonnie? I know I'm the one who said you ought to confront him, but on the other hand you shouldn't fly off the handle, either. If you lose your temper he'll have the advantage."

Bonnie stopped her pacing and turned toward Spencer. "Do you think so? I know I have to do something about Kenny. But what if it's too late? Maybe he's too firmly entrenched here, and I'll never get my inn back."

He was moved by the note of panic in her voice, in her eyes. "It's never too late to be honest with someone about how you feel," he reassured her, thinking of his own lack of honesty and hoping he was right. "I used to teach an assertiveness training course—"

"Oh, really?" she asked. "Do you have to have any special qualifications for something like that?"

"Yeah. I taught four very attractive little sisters how to say no," he improvised quickly. Damn, he hated lying to her. He wished he'd never started. But tonight—tonight he'd set everything straight. "Listen, I've got to finish up dinner. But if you'll meet me in the bathhouse later, you can rehearse what you're going to say to Kenny...and there's something else I need to talk to you about," he added, committing himself to a confession.

"Okay," Bonnie agreed casually, her heart skipping a beat as her mind invented possibilities.

"Ten o'clock," Spencer added, just before placing his hands on her shoulders, lowering her head and claiming her lightly glossed lips for his own. Briefly.

"You taste like cayenne pepper," she whispered, then licked her lips, savoring the peculiar burning sensation. Was it from Spencer, or the pepper? "Have you been sampling the rémoulade sauce?"

He nodded. "I hope I didn't get it too hot. And speaking of hot..." He eyed her up and down, as if taking inventory, then winked at her before turning back toward the kitchen.

Bonnie felt the blood rushing to her face in a blush of pleasure. No one had ever called her *hot* before. So, it wasn't the most romantic compliment in the world, but maybe old-fashioned romance just wasn't Spencer's style. So what? There was more to a man-woman relationship than hearts and flowers—much more.

Chapter Seven

Now that she was alone with her thoughts once again, Bonnie eased herself into a chair in the empty dining room. It was still early, even after the ruckus she'd caused. When and if guests began arriving for dinner, she'd get up and help Spencer, but just for now she wanted to sit quietly and mull things over.

Unfortunately, she didn't get the chance. One of the hotel's guests, a solitary young woman Bonnie hadn't yet met, was headed for the dining room, looking lost and ill at ease.

Though she would rather have sat by herself, Bonnie decided that the neighborly thing to do was invite the woman to join her. So she caught her eye and gave her a welcoming sort of smile.

"Are you expecting someone?" the woman asked, a hopeful expression on her round face.

"No, please, have a seat," Bonnie offered. They made hasty introductions.

"I just had to come and see what all the talk was about," said the woman, whose name was Celia. Then she leaned forward slightly and whispered, "Have you seen him yet?"

Bonnie was puzzled. "Seen who?"

"Professor Guthrie! I'm dying to see what he looks like wearing an apron."

Bonnie closed her eyes until the room stopped spinning. *Professor* Guthrie?

"I, uh, don't know Professor Guthrie," she finally choked out, trying to disguise the jolt of surprise still surging through her.

Celia's eyes widened, then her hand went to her mouth. "Oh! Weren't you in his class last semester? I thought I recognized you...."

"No."

"Oops! Sorry. I'm afraid I'm not making much sense, then."

"That's all right," Bonnie returned automatically. Why was she so shocked? she wondered. The first day Spencer had introduced himself she'd suspected he was hiding something. Her suspicions had mounted steadily over the next couple of days. But as their friendship had deepened and her trust had grown, she'd pushed her suspicions aside and had gradually forgotten about them. Big mistake.

Now it was time to find out the whole truth. "So tell me about this Professor Guthrie."

"He teaches a graduate sociology class on gender roles...."

Bonnie listened with growing horror as the story unfolded of how Professor Spencer Guthrie had become a housekeeper. His presence at the inn, then, was nothing but a gigantic farce. And she was his guinea pig. Fodder for his research. Something to laugh with his students about.

Her sense of outrage grew by leaps and bounds with each of Celia's words.

"Some of the stories he tells are really funny," Celia continued. "He says the owner of the hotel is a tough boss, and that he's expected to do far more than a woman housekeeper." *He tells stories about me to his class?* she thought, fighting back tears.

"Some of the other students came to the inn to purposely give him a hard time," Celia continued, oblivious to Bonnie's roiling thoughts. "You see, if he can't keep his job till the end of the semester, it'll be really embarrassing for him. All his preaching about equality, and how men can be secretaries and women can be construction workers—it just won't hold much water if he fails as a maid. I bet he can't wait till the semester's over and he can take off his apron."

Bonnie had to get away before she lost all control. The lies! If Spencer had lied about his purpose for working at the inn, what else had he lied about? Was their entire relationship based on deceit?

She abruptly complained of a headache to Celia and escaped upstairs.

Her room was no refuge, however, for the tormenting thoughts continued to plague her. Spencer was using her, she fumed, stripping off the silk dress and tossing it onto the floor of her closet. Using her to bolster his own career. She'd no doubt be written up in some journal of sociology next month, long after he'd left here and relegated her to a corner of his mind where he stored old research materials.

He *was* leaving, of course. At last she let herself acknowledge that fact, and the tears she'd held back overflowed from her eyes and down her cheeks in a torrent. The semester was over in two weeks. By then he would have made his point. There'd be no reason for him to continue working as a maid.

Just this afternoon he'd practically promised that he'd be sticking around for some time. Another lie.

Spencer couldn't help but notice Bonnie's absence as he served the shrimp rémoulade. When he saw Celia Fredericks, he felt a faint suspicion that gradually turned to certainty with each passing minute Bonnie failed to reappear. A cold brick of fear lodged somewhere next to his heart.

When he'd finished serving the pie, he slid into the chair across from Celia. She looked up, surprised.

"Did you blow my cover?" he demanded point-blank.

"Your cover?"

"Did you tell Bonnie Chapman who I am and why I'm working here?"

"B-Bonnie . . . the blond woman who was sitting here? I didn't pay much attention to her name."

"But did you tell her about me?" Spencer repeated.

"Well, yeah. I think I might have mentioned—"

Spencer didn't wait to hear the rest. He abandoned the handful of dinner guests and bounded up the stairs two at a time. Why tonight, of all nights? He had planned to come clean about the deception in less than two hours. Now, thanks to Celia, he didn't stand a chance of explaining things to Bonnie's satisfaction.

He stood outside her door, his hand poised to knock. Really, he shouldn't be blaming Celia, he decided. This was his own fault. He should have told Bonnie the truth long ago, when they first became personally—romantically—involved.

You're a fool, Spencer Guthrie, he berated himself as he worked up his courage and knocked on the door.

She was a long time answering. When she finally came to the door, she opened it only a crack and peered out with one large gray-green eye. "Yes?"

Spencer had only an impression of what she wore, cream-colored satin cascading to the floor. He had a fleeting desire to see more of it, more of her, but he marshaled his attention toward his immediate objective.

"I suppose this means I'm fired," he said.

"Fired?" A long hesitation. "No, I don't think so. That would make it too easy for you."

He was only slightly relieved. "Easy?"

"You'd go back to your class and you'd say, 'My boss found out who I was, so she fired me.' No reflection on your housekeeping abilities, no holes punched in your equality-between-the-sexes philosophy."

"Ah, now I see. You want me to quit?"

"And admit that your experiment failed," she added.

"But it hasn't. I'm a good housekeeper and I don't plan to resign."

She paused. "Then I guess there's one alternative. You'll stay...and work for Kenny."

He flinched at the harshness of her tone. He knew he deserved her anger, but she wanted him to suffer! Work for Kenny, indeed. Did she mean to make his job so miserable that he'd be forced to quit and admit defeat to his students and colleagues?

"I thought you had your mind made up to dethrone Kenny," he said.

"One crisis at a time, please."

"This doesn't have to be a crisis."

"Define it any way you like."

Spencer took a deep breath to collect his thoughts. "Bonnie, let's stop this verbal volleyball. You're obviously madder than hell, and I don't really blame you. But I'd like a chance to explain—"

She opened the door wider, giving Spencer the benefit of a full view of her slender body encased in a flowing satin nightgown, the tendrils of hair escaping from the knot at the top of her head, and her eyes, so full of accusations.

"'Mad' doesn't begin to describe how I feel, Professor Guthrie." She slammed the door in his face.

Spencer stood there for a few moments, half hoping the door would open again. When it didn't, he turned away reluctantly and, with a sinking heart, made his way back downstairs.

He woodenly refilled coffee cups and saw to the diners' last few requests before retreating into the kitchen. When the dishwasher was loaded and the last few pans were soaking in a sink of hot sudsy water, he at last allowed himself to assess his situation.

At least Bonnie hadn't fired him, he thought, trying to look on the bright side. On the other hand, she'd also made it plain that she didn't want him here. But if she thought she could force him to quit by making his job more unpleasant, she was sorely mistaken.

"You're not going to be rid of me quite that easily, Bonnie," he murmured as he scrubbed the stubborn residue inside a saucepan. If she wanted to pry him out of this hotel, she'd have to fire him…and, he mused, at last finding something to smile about, she'd find it pretty difficult to fire him if he was Super Maid.

Then he shook his head, amazed at his own thick-headedness. Holding on to his housekeeper's job didn't really matter. If he had to admit defeat to his students and swallow some of his rhetoric, he'd survive it. It was Bonnie he wanted to hold on to. She was what kept him from walking out right now. She was what had kept him at the inn all along.

"We heard Celia blew your cover," said Randy the moment Spencer walked into Mugs a few days later. "She was so embarrassed that she wouldn't even come to class today."

"Tell her I'm not mad at her," Spencer answered distractedly, motioning to the waitress for a beer as he took a seat at the large round table. "It was only a matter of time before Mrs. Chapman found out the truth, anyway." He didn't tell them about the conclusion he'd reached as a result of this grim incident. He'd decided that from now on he'd ask that his students not mislead an employer, even in the name of research. Mostly it wasn't fair to the employer, and the misunderstandings could be destructive. He'd discovered that firsthand.

"We've been talking this over," said Jenny, "and we all agree that you've completed the assignment to our satisfaction."

"Yeah, you lasted four weeks," added Vicki. "That's a lot longer than I lasted in road maintenance."

"Oh, no, I'm into my fifth week now," Spencer contradicted. "I intend to finish out the semester, just like I said I would."

"Why?" Randy looked flabbergasted. In fact, all the students did.

Why, indeed? Spencer asked himself. The students had just let him off the hook. He'd proved his point. He could quit the housekeeper's job any time he wanted with impunity. Yet he knew he'd stay on.

"I like to finish what I start," he answered with a shrug.

Bonnie sat in the clinic in Little Rock on Friday morning one week after that awful evening, trying not to squirm as Dr. Brewster used a funny little motorized saw to remove her cast. It was hard to believe that six weeks had passed since her accident. Six weeks that had thrown her life into chaotic upheaval.

She let her mind wander over the events of the past seven days, and a faint smile came to her lips as she reviewed the progress she'd made with Kenny. She was a long way from regaining control of the inn, but she did have an intelligent plan for doing so. She wasn't going to act rashly or lose her temper—Spencer was right when he'd advised her against that.

She'd decided that the practical approach was to first learn what her legal rights were. So she'd spent an afternoon in the law section of the university library. When she'd exhausted every avenue and compiled a list of questions, she'd called the lawyer in Little Rock who'd handled Sammy's estate.

Mentally she reviewed the lengthy meeting she'd had with the attorney that morning, unconsciously nodding with satisfaction. He had studied all of the papers Bonnie had gathered: wills, deeds, financial records. Bonnie hadn't fully understood everything they'd discussed concerning "tenants in common," which was apparently what she and Kenny were, but she'd gathered a nice arsenal of ammunition to use against her partner.

She now looked forward to the confrontation, for she knew she was prepared. *I'll show you assertiveness,* she mused, wondering what Spencer would think of her newfound confidence. But as the thought of Spencer flooded her mind, the faint smile died on her lips. Any way she looked at it, her efforts to straighten out that area of her life were a dismal failure.

Bonnie had wasted a lot of energy over the past week, trying to make Spencer's housekeeping job as difficult as possible so he'd be forced to resign. She'd spent her hours racking her brain for all sorts of repugnant tasks he could do, such as changing air conditioning filters, scrubbing the grout in the bathhouse, cleaning the gutters and un-clogging a drain in the basement that had been stopped up for years.

But it seemed that no matter what was demanded of him, Spencer got it done. Not only that, he did it with a smile, much to Bonnie's growing infuriation. He never complained. In fact, she often heard him whistling as he worked!

"I'm not hurting you, am I?" Dr. Brewster asked, snapping Bonnie back to the present. He'd turned her leg to an awkward angle, but she hadn't noticed.

"No, I'm fine," she answered mechanically, her thoughts already returning of their own free will to her recollections of Spencer.

This morning she'd thought perhaps he'd reached his tolerance level when she'd witnessed him through the office window battling her old vacuum cleaner. As he'd tried to empty the contents of the dust bag, an unexpected gust of wind had blown a cloud of dirt directly into his face, causing him to reel back and sneeze half a dozen times. Bonnie, who should have enjoyed his plight, had felt her own eyes watering in empathy.

In the lobby a short time later, as she'd prepared to leave for Little Rock, he'd strode toward her purposefully, a determined expression on his face.

Aha, here it comes, she'd thought as she pretended absorption in her briefcase. *He's had his quota of fun and he's going to quit.* The thought had given her little comfort.

"Mrs. Chapman?" he'd said with unnecessary formality.

"Yes?"

"I have some free time this afternoon. I noticed the shrubs in front need a trim. Would you like me to see to it?"

Her carefully monitored control had slipped then. "What kind of glutton for punishment are you?" she'd asked, dropping her battered briefcase with a thud. "I know you aren't enjoying yourself. Why do you pretend to?"

"I enjoy my job very much, ma'am," he'd replied calmly.

"Don't call me ma'am!"

"I'm sorry. I didn't know that irritated you. What would you prefer me to call you?"

"Oh, never mind. I don't care what you call me. Trim the damn bushes if it pleases you." Picking up the briefcase, she'd turned away quickly, before he could see the moisture forming in her eyes. But when she heard his footsteps moving away from her, she couldn't resist the urge to look over her shoulder at his retreating form.

"Damn you, Spencer Guthrie," she'd whispered. She'd started out wanting revenge for the hoax he'd perpetrated on her, but if watching him toil like a plow horse from dawn until late in the evening was revenge, it wasn't sweet at all.

Bonnie's plan to make him quit had backfired; he obviously wasn't going to. Instead, his presence was a constant, painful reminder of the passion that almost was, the closeness that could have been.

Yes, she could have even grown to love him—to love the man she'd believed him to be, the honest and open man, the man who'd worked at the inn because he wanted to be there.

She should have fired him when she had the chance. She'd have saved herself a lot of trouble and grief. Maybe she should just go ahead and do it now, save herself the pain of another week with him under her roof. "Maybe I will fire him," she grumbled under her breath.

"Did you say something?" Dr. Brewster asked, pausing in his efforts to free her leg from the plaster.

"Just thinking aloud," she answered distractedly.

She'd tried to convince herself that she didn't care about Spencer, but it was time for her to admit the truth. Without any conscious effort on her part—without even her knowledge—her emotions had somehow become irrevocably tangled up with his. She'd come to care about him a great deal, and she couldn't seem to stop caring, no matter how he'd deceived her.

Does he know? she wondered. Had he guessed? She hoped not. For she wasn't foolish enough to believe that any sort of reconciliation between them was possible. No, there was no way she would come out of this without scars. He would be gone in another week, but her heart would never mend as nicely as her ankle had.

When the cast was finally off, Bonnie glanced down at her leg and gasped. "It looks awful!" she exclaimed, rotating her thin white calf this way and that. "It doesn't match the other one!"

Dr. Brewster chuckled. "Don't worry, it'll return to normal once you start exercising those muscles again."

Just the same, Bonnie was glad she'd worn her favorite pair of linen slacks today, so no one would be able to view her lower leg as it made its first venture into daylight.

The doctor handed her a photocopied sheet with some exercises she could do to strengthen her weak muscles. With a final warning to take it easy, he released her, and soon she found herself headed home.

As she drove down the familiar highway toward Royal Springs, she forced herself to put Spencer out of her mind and rehearse the coming confrontation with Kenny. She felt more confident about it each time she reviewed her strategy. In some ways she felt better than she had in weeks—more in control, more sure of herself. On the other hand, she still couldn't predict Kenny's reaction, and that part made her tremble.

Kenny spotted her the moment she came through the inn's front door. He'd been sitting at the registration desk, studying a scattering of what looked like paint-color samples, but as soon as he saw Bonnie he stood and smiled toothily.

"I didn't know you were getting your cast off today," he said, moving out from behind the desk to appraise her.

"I thought I told you that this morning," she responded without any answering smile. What was he looking at paint samples for? Oh, Lord, it was a good thing she hadn't further postponed her plan to take action.

"Does your ankle still hurt?" Kenny asked in a rare moment of concern. "I mean, are you back to normal?"

"No, it doesn't hurt, but my leg muscles are awfully tired. I suppose they'll get used to the exercise soon enough."

Kenny's smile stretched even wider, if that was possible. "Great. Listen, why don't you go help Spencer clean up the last of the lunch dishes. Then I'd like to call a staff meeting in the dining room."

Bonnie's brow wrinkled. "A *staff* meeting?"

"Yeah, you know, where everyone who works here gathers and talks about things? You, me, Spencer, and Theo, too. We have some things to settle."

She thought for only a moment before retorting. "Okay, Kenny, a staff meeting it is. I myself have a few things I'd like to settle." Without bothering to acknowledge his questioning "but—" she turned and walked briskly away to find Spencer and Theo. Whatever harebrained scheme Kenny had up his sleeve, she would stop it before it started.

A few minutes later, the hotel's four principals were all seated in the dining room. Only Theo and Bonnie dared sit close enough to share one of the small square tables; Kenny and Spencer sat about as far from each other as possible.

Kenny wasted no time taking the floor. "I'm sure you're all aware that funds at the Sweetwater Inn aren't unlimited."

"Amen to that," Theo said under his breath, just loud enough that Bonnie could hear. She suppressed a smile.

Automatically her eyes sought out Spencer, to see if he shared the joke. His even gaze met hers. She saw no humor there, just a fleeting glimpse of what could only be described as pain. That pain took her by surprise, for she hadn't seen any real emotion in him since the night she'd slammed her door in his face.

"And as you all can see," Kenny continued in his most pompous voice, "Bonnie had her cast removed this morning and seems to be pretty much back to normal.

Therefore I see no reason why she can't resume the housekeeping and cooking duties. Naturally, that negates our need for Spencer's presence here. So I've taken the liberty of drawing up a check for two weeks' severance pay.''

Bonnie watched, too shocked to react, as Kenny pulled a folded check from his breast pocket and laid it on the table in front of Spencer.

Spencer didn't touch it. In fact, he made no response at all, unless you counted the slight twitching of a muscle in his jaw.

Theo was the first to break the frozen silence. ''Don't you think this decision is kinda hasty?'' he offered. ''You can't just dump all that work on Miss Bonnie when she's still recuperating.''

''Now, Theo,'' Kenny replied in a placating tone, ''Bonnie's been the housekeeper here for ten years or more. She can handle it. And if there's any real heavy work, you and I can help her with it. Right, Bonnie?''

Bonnie opened her mouth to reply, but her outrage caused her words to stick in her throat.

''Besides,'' Kenny continued, ''things will be easier for her, now that she doesn't have to worry about the complicated things like budgets and marketing, and all the planning and management tasks that I've taken over. It's an arrangement that makes a lot of sense. Bonnie and I each will be responsible for the jobs we're most suited for.''

Bonnie could feel the anger welling up inside her, displacing her calm confidence. *The jobs we're most suited for?* As if she weren't qualified to do anything except scrub floors! Because she was a woman and he was a man? Suddenly all that Spencer stood for made a tiny bit more sense to her.

She pushed her chair back slowly, forcing herself to breathe deeply, deliberately. She again remembered Spencer's advice about not losing her temper, so she warned herself not to scream, or even raise her voice. As she stood she took one final deep breath, forming her words, and started to speak.

No one heard her.

"Hold it right there, buster!" It was Spencer's words that reverberated through the room like angry thunder. Bonnie's head swiveled to look at him. He, too, had risen from his chair, but he was far from composed. In fact, every line of his body suggested anger, hostility, aggression.

Bonnie sank softly back in to her chair, stunned once again.

"I've had just about enough of watching you bully and intimidate Bonnie!" Spencer continued, waving one menacing finger in the air toward Kenny. "I tried to stay out of this, honest to God, I did, but a man can be pushed just so far. Who do you think you are, treating Bonnie like a second-class citizen? She's your business partner, not your—"

"Who do *you* think you are?" Kenny interrupted, overcoming his surprise at the sudden verbal attack. "Last time I checked, you were the maid around here—before I fired you," he added. "That gives you exactly zero authority. But to answer your question, I treat Bonnie like the kid sister she is. Let's be honest—she's hardly more than a girl, she has no education to speak of, and she'd have run the hotel right into bankruptcy if I hadn't come along. When Sammy left his half of the hotel to her, he had no intention that she should actually run things. He just wanted to make sure she was taken care of."

"By whom?" said Spencer, inching dangerously close to swinging distance from Kenny. "For five years you sure as hell weren't around to take care of her."

Bonnie could hardly believe her ears. Spencer was *defending* her, like that knight in shining armor he had once sworn he couldn't be. But just now, she wasn't a damsel in distress. For once, she knew what had to be said and what had to be done—if these loudmouthed men would let her get a word in edgewise.

"Bonnie did a heck of a good job running the Sweetwater," Theo interjected. "I don't know anyone else coulda held this place together the way she did—"

Kenny turned his attention toward the elderly maintenance man, his eyes narrowing. "Look, Theo, I can't blame you for being loyal to Bonnie. I know you two have seen some hard times together, during those years I couldn't be here to handle things. But you, if anyone, should see that a true Chapman should be running the hotel."

"And Bonnie doesn't count as one?" said Spencer, grinding out the words. "Because she merely married into the family? Never mind that she's a legal owner, or that—"

Kenny turned again, this time with a clenched fist and clenched teeth. "Look, Guthrie, I've had just about enough of this. You'd be smart to take the money and run."

"Not a chance. Not till I'm convinced Bonnie's interests are being protected."

Bonnie braced herself to take action. She'd let these pompous, self-important men waste enough time discussing her as if she were a mindless lump of clay. But how did she go about interrupting? She didn't have a prayer of being heard over their bellowing.

Abandoning her dignity, she stood on a chair, stuck her fingers into her mouth and gave an ear-piercing whistle.

One by one, each of the three men grew silent and directed his attention toward Bonnie. When the room was blessedly still, she climbed off the chair, nodded her head in thanks and walked regally to a point in the room she judged to be center stage.

They all must have sensed her quiet but very real rage, for no one spoke. In fact, Bonnie wasn't sure they were breathing.

"I've had quite enough of you men, talking about me as if I had the intelligence of a lamp." Her voice was quiet but firm, surprising even her. "Let me tell you exactly how things are going to be from now on. First of all, *you*." She turned abruptly toward Kenny. He actually flinched.

"I gave you your chance to show me what you could do. And if these are the kind of management skills they taught you in graduate school, I'm glad I didn't waste my time."

"Bonnie—" Kenny tried to interrupt.

She didn't allow him to. "Let me finish. This inn belongs to me, by virtue of five long years of hard work and hard times and my mother's life savings I spent keeping this place open while you were off gallivanting in Paris. Why do you assume you can now share in the inn's profits when you weren't around to share the risks?"

"Legally speaking—" Kenny started to say.

"Legally speaking," she repeated, "when you disappear for five years and you leave behind your property, it's called *abandonment*, and that's exactly what you did. It means you forfeit your ownership."

Kenny's mouth hung open. For once he was speechless.

"So," she continued, "as far as I'm concerned, you're the one who doesn't have any authority around here. And you certainly don't have the authority to fire Spencer."

Kenny pressed his lips into a thin line, turning once again toward Spencer. "I suppose you put her up to this?"

Spencer's eyebrows shot up and he shook his head, pleading ignorance. "I'm as surprised as you are."

"Well," said Kenny, refusing to meet Bonnie's eyes. "We'll just see about this." He turned with a huff, then made a hasty exit.

By the time Bonnie turned back toward the other two men, Theo was already making his escape through the swinging door into the kitchen.

"Chicken!" Spencer called after him as he took his chair once again.

"I don't have any quarrel with Theo," Bonnie said to Spencer. "You're the one who should have escaped when my back was turned."

"If I had any brains, I would have," he replied, barely suppressing a smile. "But some reckless part of me doesn't want to miss your encore."

His humor irritated her. This was serious business, damn it! But if he wanted to see an encore, she'd give him his wish. She placed her hands flat on the surface of the table where he sat and leaned forward until her face was just a few inches from his.

"I stopped Kenny from firing you for one reason and one reason only: so I could have the pleasure of doing so myself. Professor Guthrie, you are *fired*!"

He deserved that, she decided, and she'd felt good saying the words, as if they'd released the last of her dwindling anger toward him. Well, not the *last* of her anger, she decided when he threw back his head and laughed uproariously. At that moment she could have easily strangled him.

"Don't you dare laugh at me!" she ordered, starting to pace. "I'm serious."

Spencer struggled to master his composure. "I'm not laughing at you," he said, still with that infuriating grin. "I'm laughing out of sheer relief."

She paused her pacing long enough to look at him, confused. "Because I fired you?"

"Because you finally took control. And such control! My Lord, but you were magnificent. I *knew* you had it in you to stand up for yourself, but I had no idea you'd do it so well."

"I did do it well, didn't I?" she said, allowing herself a small smile of triumph. But her expression quickly changed to surprise as she felt herself being pulled into Spencer's lap.

"What would you say if I told you you're beautiful when you're angry?" he said.

"Oh, Spencer, puh-lease!" she said, struggling to get back on her feet. Struggling, but not very hard. "Even I know that's a sexist comment."

"Suppose I change it to 'you're beautiful whether you're angry or not'?" He gathered her close and kissed her, the way a long-lost lover would have.

Oh, the nerve! she seethed. But his lips felt like warm honey against hers—tender, caring. That was the last conscious thought she had for several long moments.

Chapter Eight

How spectacular it was to have Bonnie in his arms again, Spencer thought as he deepened the kiss, letting his tongue explore the pleasurable depths of her warm, inviting mouth. He'd begun to fear he'd never get past the barrier of coldness she'd erected behind her disinterested facade. This morning he'd deliberately goaded her, hoping to shake some reaction from her. But he'd only succeeded in making her lose her temper. He wasn't sure which was worse, her anger or her cold indifference.

Perhaps he'd finally found the correct approach, he mused as he worked his mouth against hers in a gentle assault. Bonnie wasn't too keen on listening to lengthy explanations at the moment, but she couldn't fail to understand what he was telling her with his lips and his caressing hands. She was important to him. He cared for her. He'd never meant to hurt her, and he was willing to do whatever it took to make things right between them again.

He trailed a chain of kisses along her jaw and down her neck. She tasted so good. She had an unbelievably sweet scent about her, like wildflowers and sunlight itself. He pressed his face into her thick hair and inhaled. He wanted to get naked and wrap himself in those luxuriously soft, long tresses.

He stopped himself just short of making that suggestion aloud. *Don't repeat your mistakes,* he warned himself. He had some serious apologizing to do before he could move on to impertinent suggestions that might get him into more hot water.

"You're not playing fair," Bonnie whispered into his ear just before she began to nibble on the lobe.

"I know," he acknowledged. "I couldn't think of any other way to calm you down so we could have a sensible conversation."

"I'm hardly calm," she reminded him. Her rapid breathing was testimony to the truth of her statement. "And this is not a sensible conversation."

"But at least we're talking," he said, nuzzling her neck. "Which is a definite improvement over the past week."

She sighed, though Spencer wasn't sure whether that was a sign of pleasure or irritation. "Are we going to talk, or kiss?" she asked. "Let's do one or the other. If we're going to talk, I need a clear head, and I can't keep a clear head when you're doing... *that*."

The choice should have been easy for Spencer. This might be his one and only chance to explain, to apologize. Of course he was sorely tempted to just keep holding her, too. But in the end he gathered together his willpower, placed his hands around her slim waist and lifted her off his lap. She made only a tiny huff of protest as he sat her in a chair, a minimum of five feet from his own.

"Would you care to make any opening statements?" he asked.

Her eyes were downcast as she replied. "Yes. I'd like to say—" she hesitated, then rushed on "—that I'm sorry for the way I acted over the past week. I was being vindictive and . . . and childish. But in my own defense, my self-confidence had taken quite a beating, and I was finding it difficult to face my problems squarely."

"I deserved everything you dished out, and more," said Spencer softly. "I shouldn't have lied to you. But Bonnie, please believe me, I didn't start out intending to deceive you. It all seemed innocent in the beginning. I was here merely to observe, and to prove to my graduate students that I was capable of taking on a traditionally opposite-gender role, just as I required them to do. I'm not sure when my behavior started taking on less-than-honorable overtones, but one day I woke up and saw this horrid lapse in honesty on my part."

"Then why didn't you fix it?" she asked, her words barely a whisper.

"I was going to tell you everything, that night when we were supposed to meet in the bathhouse. You remember, I said there was something else besides Ken that I wanted to discuss?"

She nodded. "And then Celia spilled the beans."

"Yup. Now ask me anything you'd like to know about me. I'll tell the honest truth. Anything."

She paused, as if thinking. "Okay. What exactly were you planning to do with the observations you made here?"

Ouch. He'd asked for this one. But he'd promised to be honest. "I took notes my first couple of weeks here.

Originally I'd planned to write an essay for a professional journal." He thought he saw her flinch just slightly. "But," he added quickly, "I threw the notes away a long time ago, and I don't plan to do anything with the memories of my stint as a maid except look fondly on them."

She seemed satisfied with that answer and went on to another question. "What kind of stories have you been telling your students about me?"

"About you specifically? Well, let's see... I once referred to you as a Southern belle, but that was before I really knew you. I told them how you resisted the idea of a male housekeeper. But I'm sure anything I said thereafter was highly complimentary. And," he added mischievously, "I didn't mention the fact that you're a fantastic kisser."

"Don't try to distract me," she said, casting him a warning glance when he would have moved closer to her. "Did you tell your class I was a tough boss? And that I expected you to do far more than a woman housekeeper?"

He thought for a moment. The words were familiar, but he'd never described Bonnie that way. "No. However, I believe I said that about Ken."

"Oh." She sighed again. "All right. I believe you. What started out as a harmless deception got a little out of hand. You didn't mean to lie, not really, and at one point you had every intention of telling me the truth."

"But?" Spencer asked, waiting with his heart in his throat for the other shoe to drop.

"I just have one more question. When—" Her voice cracked. She cleared her throat and began again. "When were you planning to give notice that you were leaving? Or were you just going to pull up your tent stakes and disappear when the semester was over at the end of next week?''

Spencer felt like slapping the heel of his hand against his forehead. Now he understood why she was so very hurt and angry. She'd assumed that he was leaving her, abandoning her to face her problems with Ken alone.

"The truth of the matter, Bonnie, is that I had no intention of leaving. If I had, I would have given you two weeks' notice. That's what I require my students to do."

Bonnie's eyebrows drew together in confusion. "You mean you were just going to keep working here? As a maid?''

"I hadn't thought it through, to be honest. All I can tell you is I had no plans to leave. I couldn't let you battle Ken by yourself, and I certainly wouldn't have offered my support if I'd intended to withdraw it. Besides,'' he added in a softer tone of voice, "I like it here.''

She crossed her arms over her chest. "Housework fulfills you?''

"C'mon, Bonnie, you know what I'm trying to say. Housework is all right, in moderation. You're the reason I don't want to leave.''

"Oh." Her eyelashes fluttering a bit, she wouldn't meet his gaze.

"But," he continued, shrugging his shoulders, "if I'm fired, I'm fired. I'll fade away gracefully." He started to rise.

She looked up quickly. "Oh, no, you don't! You're officially *unfired*. You can't leave. Now that I've started this battle with Kenny, I feel like I've grabbed hold of a copperhead by the tail. If I'm going to finish the job I need some moral support.''

Spencer arched one eyebrow at her as he stood. "Is that the only reason you want me around?''

That finally coaxed a small smile out of her. She stood also. "Course not. You're a darn good maid. Have we done enough talking yet?"

He breathed a sigh of contentment as she slipped easily into his embrace. She was evading his question, but he let her get away with it. Maybe she wasn't ready to admit that she just plain wanted him to stick around, but he knew she did. Or rather, he hoped she did.

Seems like old times, Bonnie thought happily as she sat at the kitchen counter, peeling a couple of dozen boiled eggs for dinner. Spencer was washing and slicing a sinkful of vegetables from the garden. Somehow, in all the uproar, everyone had forgotten about sixteen guests who might show up for dinner. The Cornish game hens Kenny had dictated for this evening's menu weren't even thawed, so Bonnie and Spencer were hastily throwing together hearty chef's salads.

"I think we can pull off some hot fudge sundaes for dessert," Spencer suggested. "I doubt Ken will be around to object."

"No, I imagine he went running straight to a lawyer to find out if what I said was true."

"Is it?" Spencer asked. "You had me convinced."

"It all depends on how you look at it," Bonnie answered as she began slicing the peeled eggs. "Theoretically, according to my attorney, I owe Kenny half of the inn's profits over the past five years."

"Really? That's awful."

"However, over the past five years there was no profit. The hotel is still recovering from the losses. So in actuality, Kenny owes me for half of all my own money I invested, plus half the additional monies the business lost, plus half of whatever my work as a manager and house-

keeper is deemed to be worth. It's a little more complicated than I'm making it sound, but what it works out to
is that Kenny owes me several thousand dollars."

"Now that's more like it. How does this 'abandonment' business fit in?" Spencer asked.

"I can argue that he abandoned the property for five
years and showed no interest in the welfare of the business, and if I succeed with that argument his half of the
hotel could revert back to me. But I doubt Kenny would
let that happen without a nasty court battle."

"Would you go that far?" Spencer asked.

Bonnie pursed her lips. "Yes, I guess I would. I love
this old place. It didn't belong to my ancestors, but it's
the only real home I've ever known. I can't let Kenny de-
stroy it."

With the unexpected swiftness of a tornado, the stress
and pain of her rivalry with Kenny caught up with her
then. She bent her head over the boiled eggs and squeezed
her eyes shut, willing the tears away. She'd never cried in
front of Spencer—or in front of anyone, except maybe
Theo, for a very long time. She didn't want to start now.

She cursed silently as first one eye overflowed with
tears, then the other. Only a few minutes ago she'd begun to believe she could be that strong, self-reliant
woman Spencer wanted her to be. Now this. A complete
nervous breakdown, and no way to have it in privacy.

She tried to take a quiet, deep breath. It turned into a
noisy gasp.

Spencer whirled around to look at her. "Bonnie?" He
was beside her in an instant. "What happened? What's
wrong?"

She shied away from the comforting touch he instinctively offered. "I'm...okay," she managed between sobs.

"Don't . . . worry about me. I'll be . . . fine in a m-minute or two."

He ignored her protests and pulled her against him, smoothing her hair with his hand as he would a frightened child. "Come on, sweetheart, just let it all out," he murmured. "Everything's going to work out. You'll see."

It felt wonderful to lean her moist cheek against his warm, solid chest, to let his arm encircle her shoulders in such a protective way. Part of her wanted to relax and give in to his comforting. She fought that urge, however, because she knew what Spencer must be thinking—that she was weak, that she'd never be able to stand up to a full-fledged legal battle against Kenny.

He must despise these tears! she thought, but the more she tried to shut them off the more she cried. It was hopeless. She simply couldn't be the strong sort of woman Spencer would love and respect. Those moments they'd spent in each other's arms earlier that afternoon were wonderful, but she was deluding herself if she believed a few kisses could lead to a permanent relationship. And that was what she wanted for herself and Spencer. She wouldn't settle for less.

The more she thought about it the more miserable she became, until she was crying for all sorts of reasons apart from the fatigue and stress that had started her on this jag in the first place.

"Would you just relax and let it all out?" Spencer asked for the third time. "That's what shoulders are made for. Now quit trying to pull away."

Bonnie sniffed loudly. "But you shouldn't have to—"

"I don't have to, I want to. It's all right to cry, sweetheart."

"N-no it's not. I'm acting like a sniveling crybaby."

"But you were strong when it counted."

Why couldn't he understand? she thought as she surrendered and slumped against him. Right now was what counted. Spencer was the one who'd made her discover the strength in herself. What was the point if she couldn't at least put on a brave front for him?

But he was so strong himself, so warm and reassuring, that she let him hold her and stroke her until she was able to absorb some of his calm and the sobbing subsided.

"Feel better?" he asked, finally turning her loose.

"I feel mortified," she said softly as she moved away from him. "This wasn't supposed to happen." She made a quick escape out the swinging doors.

Spencer watched her go, his heart overflowing with tenderness and compassion for her. He'd seen plenty of people cry—men, women and children—but no tears had ever moved him as Bonnie's had. And they weren't a sign of weakness, as she seemed to believe. She was risking a lot with this campaign against her brother-in-law, and new risk meant new levels of stress and fear. She wouldn't be human if she didn't feel like crying, especially after all that had happened today.

He wished now that he'd told her that, he thought as he began to assemble the salads. But he'd been too busy trying to sort out his own muddled feelings, trying to deal with his urge to protect her, shelter her and solve her problems for her.

He'd already jumped to her rescue once today, a gesture that was completely out of character for him, and totally unnecessary to boot. She didn't need him to be her champion. Why, then, did some inner part of him keep forcing these Sir Galahad tendencies into the open?

He'd never known a woman who could fry his logic so easily. This need he felt to rescue Bonnie went against everything he'd studied and taught for the past umpteen years. How could a relationship with her be healthy when her mere presence could shake the foundations of what his whole career stood for?

"Oh, blast it," he muttered. He could always start a new career. But a woman like Bonnie appeared only once in a man's lifetime.

A couple of days later Spencer was polishing the registration desk when he overheard Ken talking on the phone. The door to the office was ajar, and Ken was making no effort to lower his voice.

"I told you I don't have it yet! If you'll just keep your pants on, I'm working on it. You've waited five years to catch up with me, you can wait a few more weeks!"

Spencer didn't think much about it until later that afternoon as he was sweeping and dusting Ken's room. He was going after the dust bunnies under the bed with his broom when he hit a solid object, a box, which tipped over and spilled. Laying down the broom, he attempted to scoop the contents of the box back inside when he realized he was holding letters from Bonnie to Ken. The top three were dated within the past couple of months.

He didn't do anything so gauche as read the letters. Just looking at the postmarks constituted snooping, he thought with a twinge of guilt. But the postmarks led him to at least one conclusion: Ken had lied to Bonnie. He'd claimed not to have received any letters from her in two or three years, and yet here was evidence to the contrary. He claimed to have returned to Royal Springs to bring the Sweetwater Inn back to its former status, yet he'd obviously known all along that Bonnie was already starting to make a profit.

Why was Ken Chapman really here?

Spencer closed the box of letters, then returned it to where he'd found it. Hastily he completed the dusting, all the while mulling over various possibilities. In light of the phone call he'd overheard, the conclusion he came up with was the only one that made sense.

He knew he had to tell Bonnie, but he wasn't looking forward to the task.

He found her weeding the garden, her long cotton skirt hitched up to midthigh so that her extended legs could catch the morning sun. He had to smile when she caught sight of him and quickly tucked her legs under her.

"Your leg can't look that bad," he chided her, having a seat on the grass at the edge of the garden.

"Trust me, it does," she replied with a grimace. "But it won't for long. What can I do for you?" Her manner toward him had been friendly but cautious ever since the crying bout, as if she weren't quite sure where they stood anymore. He'd taken his cues from her, resisting the urge to push. She'd been through a lot, he kept telling himself. She needed time to readjust, to get to know him again under the new circumstances.

He needed time, too, to think things through, to decide in a rational manner where, if anywhere, he wanted this relationship to go. Unfortunately, he couldn't manage to do much thinking. All his thoughts were occupied with images of Bonnie, the way she looked when her eyes went all smoky with desire, the way she felt when he held her, all soft and womanly, the way she smelled—

"Spencer?"

He snapped back to the present. Why did he need to daydream when she was sitting three feet away from him?

"I just wanted to talk to you about Ken," he said. "How are things going, by the way?" He already knew the answer to that, but he wanted to hear her assessment of the situation.

Bonnie wrinkled her nose, her cheerful expression vanishing immediately. "He won't back down. He's practically barred me from the office and he refuses to discuss anything. There doesn't appear to be any room for compromise or negotiation." She took a deep breath. "I'm going ahead with a lawsuit."

Spencer wished he could do something to take the pain out of her eyes. He had a feeling what he was about to say would only add to it. "I know what a tough decision that was for you to make. But I was wondering—maybe there's one more alternative, one tactic you haven't tried."

"Such as?"

"Have you ever asked yourself why Ken came back to Royal Springs?"

Bonnie shrugged. "I thought at first that it was just as he said—that he was homesick, that he wanted to help me. But those reasons don't make much sense anymore. I'm more inclined to believe he's in it for money."

Spencer breathed a sigh of relief. He hadn't wanted to point out that possibility. He told Bonnie about the phone call and the letters, and she reacted more calmly than he'd expected.

"That only reinforces what I've begun to find out about Kenny. The lawyer put in a call to the textile company where Kenny worked in Paris. Apparently he was fired some time ago under questionable circumstances."

Spencer winced. If Ken had been unemployed for some time, he *had* to be in need of money, which fit in all too conveniently with their theory.

"But why, if he wanted to make money, was he constantly *spending* money? The reupholstering, the wallpaper, the gourmet food..."

Bonnie shrugged. "He probably took one look at the books and realized this place was hardly the gold mine he'd hoped to find. He did try to make money on the chandelier. But as for the rest of his crazy ideas, I honestly believe he thought the changes he made would bring in more customers and more money. Simple mathematics should have told him he couldn't increase profits that way, but—" she shrugged again "—he's the one with the business degree."

"Let's assume he did return here for monetary gain," he said. "There's one easy way to get rid of him."

Bonnie laughed, apparently reading his thoughts. "Spencer, if I had two dimes of my own to rub together, I'd offer to buy him out in a second. And I think he'd probably agree. But all my money is tied up in the inn."

"What about a bank loan?"

She shook her head. "The local bank won't lend me a penny. They're convinced I'm a bad risk. And frankly, just looking at the financial statements, no bank is going to lend me money, not until I have a more consistent track record."

That pretty effectively shot down his idea, Spencer thought irritably. Damn. He'd thought for sure he'd come up with the solution to Bonnie's problem.

"You don't have to look so glum," she said. "I've got a pretty good shot at winning in court, if it comes to that."

"I just wish you didn't have to sue your own brother-in-law."

"I don't like it, either, but it's the right thing to do. I'm doing it for Sammy, and his father, and his grandfather, and all the Chapmans who cared for this place along the way.''

When he heard the note of wistfulness in her voice, he looked at her sharply, hoping against hope that she wasn't losing faith. But then, unexpectedly, she smiled boldly as if wishing to reassure him.

"It's hot," she said, effectively dismissing the subject of Ken. "A perfect day to play hooky from our chores and pay a visit to the swimming hole."

Say no, Spencer warned himself. He remembered all too precisely what Bonnie looked like in a bikini, and he wasn't sure he could be trusted to comport himself as a gentleman. *Say no.* "You have a swimming hole?" he asked.

"A wide place in the creek. It's deep, and cold, and heaven on a day like this. Come on," she cajoled, reading the uncertainty in his eyes.

Impulse won out against common sense. He jumped to his feet and said quickly, before he could change his mind again, "I'll meet you back here in five minutes."

Bonnie had to laugh as she pushed herself up onto her own feet and shook the garden dirt from her clothes. She adored Spencer when he got that mischievous gleam in his eye and abandoned his proper employee's demeanor.

Being this man's boss was definitely a disadvantage, she decided. She'd have to think of a way to change his status and yet keep him around. But that was too much of a challenge at the moment. For just this afternoon, she wouldn't think about all the things that drove her crazy. She'd concentrate on the impossible attraction she felt for one man, who had to be the most improbable romantic partner for her in the world, but who she'd come to realize was the only one she wanted.

He was waiting for her by the time she'd put a swim-suit on under her clothes and returned to the back porch. He took her hand in a sweet, gentle gesture of friendship and they set off for the woods. The creek was less than a ten-minute walk from the hotel. They made a cautious path down the steep bank and waded upstream for a bit until they came to the wide deep water where Bonnie had spent so many summer days as a child.

It was a beautiful, almost enchanted spot, sheltered by limestone walls and towering pines, and a tire swing that hung from fifty feet up. The place echoed with Bonnie's carefree childhood memories of herself, Sammy and Kenny, which was one reason she hadn't visited the swimming hole in a long time. It used to make her sad, remembering those happy times that were forever lost to her. Today, however, with Spencer's reassuring presence at her side, she could smile at the recollections.

"It's time to make new memories here," she mur-mured.

Spencer was already climbing onto the bank and stripping off his clothes. Bonnie took several heart-stopping moments to appreciate his dangerously male body. Then she gave her mismatched legs only one more passing thought before shimmying out of her skirt. "Wait," she called out, "before you jump in, there's a certain ritualistic procedure you have to follow."

"Or what?" he asked, obviously amused.

"Or you're a lily-livered chicken and you can't be a member of the club."

"All right, I'm game. What's the procedure?"

"You have to climb up to the third branch of that oak tree and swing out on the tire. When the swing is at its very highest point over the water, *then* you jump."

Spencer skeptically eyed first the tree, then the swing. "You sure about this? How deep is the water?"

"Yes, I'm sure. And it's about seven or eight feet deep—if you jump at the right place," she said as she unbuttoned her cotton blouse to reveal the modest red one-piece.

Spencer didn't answer as he studied her for a few breathless seconds. "You go first," he finally said.

"Okay." She smiled confidently as she scaled the tree as agilely as a monkey, pleased that for once she could be braver than him. She could perform this acrobatic feat in her sleep. She caught the swing's rope with a dead branch and brought it to her, all the while watching Spencer out of the corner of her eye. He studied the process with obvious interest.

"Watch out for your ankle," he warned as she hooked her legs over the top of the tire.

"I'll be careful," she called back. "Geronimo!" She let go of the tree and swung out, laughing delightedly. It was just like flying, she thought as she let go at precisely the right moment, making a graceful feet-first plunge into the middle of the creek. Spencer was applauding her when she surfaced.

"Your turn," she called to him, pushing her wet hair out of her face.

"Not a chance," he said, executing a swimmer's dive across the surface of the creek. In two long strokes he was at her side. "That tire-swing stuff is the kind of trick that if you don't learn it as a child you'll never learn it. I'd break my neck."

"Lily-livered chicken," she said under her breath. "You'll never know what you're missing."

"Broken bones," he replied. Then abruptly he disappeared under the water.

When he didn't reappear after several moments, Bonnie looked around worriedly. "Spencer?"

A pair of strong arms grabbed her around the hips and pulled her under. With practiced ease she slipped out of his grasp and resurfaced a few feet away, laughing. "I feel just like a kid again," she said between giggles when he came up for air. "I haven't had this much fun in years."

"Ah, but you don't look like a kid," he said in a low voice.

She recognized that predatory gleam in his eye, and it gave her a pure thrill of feminine delight. Just when she'd begun to think they were destined to be only friends after all, he turned her world topsy-turvy with that look.

She led him a merry chase around the swimming hole, for she was a strong swimmer and could hold her breath underwater for a long time. But in the end he caught her, or she let him catch her, she wasn't sure which. They stood in waist-deep water, wet limbs entwined around each other, laughing giddily. In the next second their smiles faded and their lips met hungrily. The kiss they shared was all the more intense after the breathless pursuit.

Despite the coolness of the water, Bonnie thought she was on fire. Spencer's hands seemed to be everywhere at once—in her hair, caressing her breasts, cupping her derriere to bring them even closer together.

"Oh, Spencer," she breathed against his demanding lips. "I wish I knew what was going on with us."

He pulled back then, seeming to catch his breath. He moved his hands to her shoulders, letting his thumbs caress the slender column of her neck. "Would it make you feel any better to know that I'm at least as confused as you?"

"I'm not sure," she answered, smiling impishly. "I think it might help if at least one of us knew where we were headed. But just when I think I have things figured out, something goes haywire. There have been so many hurdles and pitfalls in our paths lately. I'd intended to forget all my problems this afternoon, but I didn't succeed." She was thinking out loud now, not quite sure where she might end up. "Maybe if we hadn't had so many disasters to deal with at once, we wouldn't have let things between us...drift with the tide. Am I making sense?"

"In a way." He eyed her speculatively.

"I've let circumstances push me around until I don't know what I want anymore."

"And I'm just confusing you further?"

She shook her head. "I'm confusing myself, talking in circles like this. I just wish someone would hand me a Swiss bank account. Then I could buy Kenny out. He'd run off to Paris or someplace, and things could return to normal. *Then* maybe I could make more sense out of you and me."

She looked up at Spencer for some sign that he knew what she was talking about. But his eyes seemed to be focused at some point just above her left eyebrow. "Spencer?"

Several long moments passed before he returned his gaze to her. But even then, she saw a sort of distant look in his eyes, as if his mind were on anything but her, or what she'd been saying.

"Why didn't I think of this before?" he asked rhetorically, more to the trees than to her.

"Think of what?"

"It makes so much sense. It would solve seven or eight problems all at once."

"What would? Spencer, what are you talking about?" she asked, puzzled at his strange behavior.

When he finally did look at her, really look at her, he was smiling triumphantly. He gripped her shoulders almost painfully. "I've got to go. Do you think you can handle the housework and cooking for a couple of days?"

"Well, yes, but—"

"Great. I'll explain everything later. Right now I've got to move, take action, before I regain my sanity and change my mind." He was already wading to the shore.

"Spencer, you aren't making a bit of sense," she said. "I'm beginning to think you really have lost your mind."

"That's a distinct possibility." He pulled his T-shirt over his head. "But I'm sure it's just a temporary condition. Can you get back to the inn by yourself? Your ankle isn't bothering you, is it?"

"My ankle's fine," she answered, heading for the shore. "Just wait, I'm coming with you."

"There's no time." He zipped up his shorts over his wet bathing suit, then slipped into his tennis shoes. He was already striding away by the time Bonnie waded up on shore. "But don't worry," he called over his shoulder, "everything's going to work out great. I have a plan that will solve all our problems."

A plan for *what*? she wanted to scream after him, but she sensed that further demands on her part wouldn't elicit any answers. She watched him leave, feeling more confused than ever. She'd obviously done something to set him off, but she couldn't for the life of her figure out what it was.

"This relationship," she muttered as she stood dripping on the creek bank, "has more ups and downs than the Ozark Mountains."

Chapter Nine

Spencer found Ken in the lobby, pacing in circles around the chair and love seat Norm had returned that morning, sans new upholstery.

"Do you know anything about this?" he demanded before Spencer could open his mouth.

Spencer shrugged. "I guess Bonnie didn't want new furniture."

"And I suppose what I want doesn't matter?" Ken challenged, as if Spencer were somehow responsible for the furniture.

Spencer resisted the urge to retort. He had a delicate mission ahead of him, and provoking Kenny any further wouldn't serve his purposes. "Ken," said Spencer smoothly, "I have a business proposition for you. Can we go into the office and discuss it?"

"What is it?" Ken snapped. "I know you're not crazy enough to ask *me* for a raise."

Spencer nodded toward the office. "If you'll just give me a few minutes, I think you'll be interested in what I have to say."

Apparently Ken's curiosity got the best of him. He sauntered into the office ahead of Spencer, closed the door behind them, then sat self-importantly behind his desk.

In less than twenty minutes, Spencer had the answer he needed from Kenny. They shook hands—quickly, as if each feared the other had some communicable disease—and Spencer went to pack his bags.

Bonnie took her time in returning to the inn. She ambled through the woods, oblivious to the rustling leaves and the breeze that hinted of rain, as she tried to sort out her thoughts. By the time she arrived home, Spencer was gone. His car was gone. She couldn't resist peeking into his room. The uncharacteristic disarray hinted at a rushed departure.

Don't panic, her rational half warned. Spencer had told her he was leaving and that he'd be back. There was no reason to fear that he wouldn't return. She could cope with his absence for a couple of days.

"You'd think I'd never run the inn alone," she chided herself as she headed for the front desk. She'd have to consult the reservations book and make sure all the rooms were made up. Not that she anticipated any problems. Spencer might have left in a hurry, but he was too conscientious to leave his work half-finished.

He surprised her on that count. Theo caught up with her just as she was heading up the stairs to check the rooms. "I've been looking for you," he said. "Spencer left this for you." He pulled a small envelope out of the pocket of his overalls. "After you read that, I'd appreciate it if you'd tell me what the heck's goin' on around here. There're some strange doin's.''

''Oh?'' Bonnie settled down on one of the steps and fingered the envelope nervously, but she resisted opening it.

''Well, for starters,'' Theo explained, leaning against the stair railing, ''Spencer tore out of here a few minutes ago like the seat of his pants was on fire. And Kenny— well, he *smiled* at me. He's been strutting around like a banty rooster and grinning ear to ear.''

''I honestly don't know what's going on,'' said Bonnie as she tore open the envelope. ''Maybe this will give us a clue.'' She scanned the brief note. Disappointed, she handed it to Theo. What had she expected, poetry? From Spencer?

Theo read aloud.

''Dear Bonnie,
Cornish game hens for dinner are thawing. Recipe's on the counter. Rooms 204 and 205 need to be made up. Last load of sheets is in the dryer. Will explain when I get back.

Spencer.''

Theo looked at her quizzically.

She shrugged. ''I guess we'll find out what's going on sooner or later.''

''Humph, I'm beginning to think I'd be better off not knowing,'' Theo grumbled as he made his way back down the stairs. ''I've had enough surprises lately.''

Spencer telephoned Bonnie that night. The connection was bad and his voice sounded scratchy, but it was music to her ears. ''Where are you?'' she asked.

"I'm taking care of some personal business that simply couldn't wait. Is everything all right at the inn?"

Was it? Bonnie asked herself. "I suppose," she answered aloud. "Kenny's acting funny, though."

"How so?"

"He's smiling. And he didn't make one critical comment during dinner. I'm hoping it's a good sign, like maybe he's finally decided that we can be partners after all."

"Don't count on it," said Spencer cryptically. "I'll see you in a couple of days." He hung up.

Bonnie replaced the receiver gently onto the phone, feeling more confused than ever. "I'll just take things as they come," she resolved aloud. For all she knew, Spencer was in Las Vegas, catering to a gambling habit, or paying his respects to a dying relative, or indulging in a rendezvous with a long-neglected lover. Then she stopped and laughed at herself. It was time to put her insecurities aside and trust Spencer. Whatever he was doing, it had something to do with the situation at the Sweetwater Inn. But all the speculation in the world wouldn't tell her any more than she already knew. She'd just have to wait and see.

Two days stretched into three, and three into four. Bonnie heard no further word from Spencer, and her doubts preyed on her mercilessly. Was he *ever* going to return? Maybe she'd scared him off, with all her hints about wanting to straighten out their relationship and her wishy-washy state of mind.

She'd come to depend on him too much, she decided when she found herself purposely avoiding Kenny, lest there should be some sort of disagreement. She felt less equipped to assert herself now that Spencer wasn't here, though realistically she knew that was silly. He might have inspired her to stand up to Kenny, but she'd done the standing up all by herself.

The only bright spot in her life at the moment was that she and Kenny weren't disagreeing. In fact, he was more agreeable than she'd seen him since his return from Paris.

She'd never get these men figured out!

Spencer held his breath as he opened the front door of the inn. He'd been gone five days—much longer than he'd intended. But, unfortunately, that was how long it had taken to get his finances straightened out.

"Come right this way, Mrs. Tilden," he addressed the matronly woman whom he'd brought with him from town, and with whom he'd spent most of the afternoon. "Have a seat in the lobby. Both Ken's and Bonnie's cars are here, so this shouldn't take too long."

"Spencer?"

He looked up to the welcome sight of Bonnie as she made her way down the staircase, dressed in blue walking shorts and matching high-top tennis shoes. He took the time to appreciate her legs, *both* her legs, now that they matched again. Her slightly funky outfit didn't mitigate her goddesslike image to Spencer; neither did the bucket of cleaning supplies dangling from one hand.

Her eyes lit up with welcome. "I thought I heard your voice." She left the cleaning supplies sitting on the bottom step, forgotten, as she hurried to Spencer. He was there to meet her, arms outstretched. He pulled her close, squeezed tight, then brushed his lips over hers.

"I missed you," he whispered.

"Me, too," she whispered back. "Oh, Spencer, I know this is silly, but you were gone so long I was half-afraid you weren't coming back."

He grinned wickedly in response. "I haven't earned your trust yet, huh?" Then he reached around and gave her a playful swat on her behind. "What were you thinking? Of course I was coming back. Things just took longer than I expected."

"What things?" she asked breathlessly. "Are you going to tell me what's going on, or do I have to break your—oh, I'm sorry." Her eyes had focused on Mrs. Tilden, who sat in the Victorian love seat, eyeing the proceedings with interest.

"Hello, Bonnie, dear," the older woman said as she stood up to greet her hostess. "It's been a while since I've run into you at the church. You are planning to contribute to the Fall Bake Sale, of course?"

"Wouldn't miss it for the world," Bonnie replied, frantically cataloguing all the reasons Francis Tilden would be paying her a visit. Not because of the bake sale; that could be accomplished with a phone call.

"Where's Ken?" Spencer asked, an anticipatory gleam in his eye. "We have to have a meeting."

"A staff meeting?" Bonnie wrinkled her nose, wondering if she could handle the stress of another one.

"More or less. You, me, Ken—and Mrs. Tilden."

Bonnie gave Spencer a puzzled frown. "What for? What's going on?"

"I'll explain it all shortly, I promise."

She had no choice but to trust him. "All right," she answered, though with a shade of uncertainty. "I'll see if I can't scare up Kenny. But I hope you aren't going to spring any big surprises on me. My nerves are tight as banjo strings."

In answer Spencer gave her another enigmatic grin.

A terrible suspicion occurred to Bonnie as she wandered around the inn, trying to locate Kenny. Was Spencer going to propose that Mrs. Tilden replace him as housekeeper? Was this meeting just a prelude to his final departure?

Somehow, though, Bonnie couldn't picture the dignified Mrs. Tilden as a maid. She was a wealthy widow, an energetic club-woman type who often donated her time to various charitable concerns. She also worked as a legal secretary for a local lawyer, Bart Bartholomew.

A *legal* secretary. Was Kenny filing a countersuit against her? Was Mrs. Tilden here in an official capacity?

You're letting your imagination run away again, she chided herself as she made her way along the covered walkway toward the bathhouse. If Mrs. Tilden was here to talk about a lawsuit, Spencer wouldn't have been grinning like a Cheshire cat.

The bathhouse was the last place she could think of to look for Kenny. Sure enough, she found him there. He wasn't soaking in one of the pools, but was sitting on a crumbling stone bench, staring into space. Bonnie had to tap him on the shoulder to gain his attention.

"What? Oh, it's you."

"What are you doing in here?" she couldn't help asking.

"Just thinking . . . about when we were kids, and how we used to play in here. Remember when Sammy and I had you convinced there was a secret tunnel that led from the Lovers' Pool to the swimming hole? You spent a whole day trying to find the magic door."

"I never did figure out how you all tricked me. I can still remember seeing Sammy disappear from that pool, and then reappear from under the water at the swimming hole."

Kenny smiled, a genuine smile that softened Bonnie's hardened heart and forced her to remember the mischievous child Kenny once had been. "Maybe it was magic," he said softly. "It's only been over the last few days that I've let myself remember how it was, when Sammy was alive. The inn itself really hasn't changed much... but everything else has."

"Don't do this to me, Kenny," she said, stiffening her spine and taking an instinctive step backward. "Don't go all warm and fuzzy and nostalgic on me. Because I'm not going to back down. I won't let you take over the inn without a fight."

"I hope we won't have to fight anymore," he said, staring off into space pensively. Abruptly he glanced up at her, grounded in reality once again. "Did you come here looking for me?"

"Oh." Bonnie had all but forgotten her reason for seeking Kenny out in the first place. "Spencer wants to meet with us."

"Spencer's back? Great. Now we can get on with things." He stood without delay and strode purposefully out of the bathhouse. Bonnie followed, shaking her head in dismay. Apparently everyone knew what was going on except her. Things were getting more and more weird.

By the time Bonnie and Kenny seated themselves onto opposite ends of the camelback sofa in the living room, Mrs. Tilden was already settled into a wing chair. Bonnie, now feeling a bit like *Alice in Wonderland*, watched with curiosity as the older woman laid out stacks of official-looking papers on the antique cherry wood coffee table. Spencer stood nervously at her elbow, also watching the proceedings but with obvious eagerness.

"All right," Bonnie said decisively, "it's time some-one filled me in."

"You mean, you boys haven't told her what you're up to?" said Mrs. Tilden, shaking her finger in mild reproach.

"We wanted to surprise her," Spencer explained. "Bonnie, I've offered to buy Ken's half of the inn and he's agreed. Mrs. Tilden is here on behalf of the law firm handling the transaction."

Bonnie's mouth dropped open. She tried to speak, but the only noise she could make was a shocked gasp.

"Naturally we need your permission before the deal can go through," Kenny added.

"But I've already drawn all the papers up," said Mrs. Tilden in a reassuring voice. "All you have to do is sign a few forms and I can process Mr. Guthrie's offer. And if all goes well, we can close in a couple of weeks."

This *is* like *Alice in Wonderland*, Bonnie thought as she looked into first one pair of expectant eyes and then another. Her head was spinning crazily. She finally locked in on Spencer. "Why?" she managed to ask.

He shrugged with an irritating nonchalance. "Because I want to. It's a good investment."

Her head swiveled toward Kenny. "And you agree?" Her voice sounded distressingly squeaky.

"I've decided to go back to Paris," he answered with a sheepish grin. "I belong to the Sweetwater Inn's past, not her future."

She looked back at Spencer, hoping he would offer her some additional clue. His face was animated with optimism, but he gave no further explanations.

Bonnie knew she should be elated, she thought dazedly. But somehow she couldn't manage more than a distracted smile. She took the pen someone had thrust at her, held it in a death grip and started to sign on the dotted line Mrs. Tilden had indicated. But she paused midway through her first name.

"Are you sure about this?" she asked Spencer.

"Positive."

She turned to Kenny once again. "And you?"

He nodded.

"But . . ." She couldn't think of a single logical objection, though she knew there must be at least one. She made another false start with the pen, then calmly laid it down. "I can't do this just yet."

"Why not?" Spencer and Kenny asked together.

"This is an important step, one that will affect me for the rest of my life." She stood and began to pace. "I can't take it lightly. I can't just sign this paper because all of you think I should. I need some time to think."

Mrs. Tilden cleared her throat nervously. "I'll just leave these papers here for you to review, Bonnie," she said. "If you have any questions you can call Bart. I'll see myself out." Obviously sensing the tension, she retreated through the French doors.

"I don't get it, Bonnie," Kenny said, after the front door had closed. "You'd file a lawsuit to be rid of me, but you won't take an easy way out when one's offered to you." He stormed out of the room, shaking his head.

Not trusting her wobbly knees to hold her up much longer, Bonnie sank back onto the sofa.

Spencer sat down cautiously in the chair across from her. "You're not pleased?" he asked.

"I . . . I'm just so surprised . . . no, shocked is a better word. And touched that you would do something like this. What in the world made you . . . I mean, *why*? To rescue the maiden in distress is just not like you."

Spencer shrugged, as if this were no big deal. "I told you, it's a good investment. Anyway," he added, averting his eyes, "you need rescuing."

"But I don't," Bonnie objected. "Now, don't get me wrong," she added quickly. "It's not that I don't appreciate your astoundingly generous gesture. I mean, it's not every day that someone offers to buy half a hotel just to get me out of a sticky situation." She paused, not quite sure how to phrase what she wanted to say.

"But?" Spencer prompted.

"But I was handling things pretty well under my own steam."

He didn't know how to respond. He'd thought she would be overjoyed that he'd solved her problem with Kenny. Her uncertainty was baffling.

"Why wouldn't you want me to buy Kenny's share of the inn?" he asked. "I could—"

"No," Bonnie said in a definite tone of voice. "Oh, Spencer, you must think I'm an ungrateful wretch. I'm really happy you want to do this, and I'm sure I'll get downright enthusiastic as soon as I get over the shock. But the idea of you and me, together, owning this hotel—well, it takes some getting used to."

"Bonnie, you're babbling." He reached across the space that separated them and took her hand. At the touch of her soft skin to his, his body stilled then leaped to life.

"Come over here and sit by me," he cajoled, his voice husky. Five days away from Bonnie had only sharpened his fascination with her, his desire for her.

She moved to the love seat, then settled against him, though somewhat stiffly. He placed a protective arm around her fragile shoulders, and she sighed. Yes, this felt right, he thought contentedly.

"As much as I hate to admit it, you're right not to make any snap decisions." He took her hand and absently stroked the back of it. "We shouldn't have tried to rush you. Let the idea sink in, and then decide."

"It seems like I ought to have some questions to ask," she said.

"I'm sure you'll think of some. In fact, why don't we go out to dinner tonight—somewhere nice. We've never done that before. You can relax and ask me all the questions you want." *And I might have a question or two to ask you,* he added silently.

"Dinner? Yes, I suppose that would be nice," she said, the corners of her mouth turning up slightly. Abruptly she frowned. "Wait, what am I thinking? We can't go out to dinner. We have our own dinner guests to worry about."

"Hang our dinner guests. We can work something out."

She looked at him sharply. "I can't afford to hang the guests. And if you plan to be a partner here, you can't hang them, either."

The way she said the word "partner," it sounded cold, Spencer thought, disturbed at her tone of voice. Actually he hadn't thought of Bonnie in terms of a business partnership. Ever since he'd come up with this idea to buy half the hotel, he'd had a much more personal alliance in mind.

"We can work something out without doing a disservice to the guests," he clarified. "We should be allowed a night out to celebrate."

"Celebrate? Isn't that a bit premature?"

"Maybe not," he ventured, determined to shake her out of this ambivalent mood of hers. "If it's too early to celebrate a partnership, perhaps we could celebrate our engagement instead.''

If he'd wanted to shake her up, he'd succeeded. She pulled away from his light embrace and turned to face him squarely, her gray-green eyes practically on fire. ''Are you serious?''

''Of course I'm serious. I wouldn't joke about a thing like that.'' Damn, he'd thought he'd just breeze in here and sweep her off her feet—solve all her problems by buying half a hotel and proposing marriage, all in one fell swoop. At the moment Bonnie Chapman was about as easy to sweep as a bag of wet cement.

''Oh. Oh!'' She took a deep breath and stood up, then started to pace. ''Do you have to hit me with this all at once? My God, Spencer, you're going to give me a nervous breakdown!''

Spencer felt as if he'd been socked in the stomach. She was saying no! He'd obviously been too sure of himself, too sure of Bonnie's feelings for him. He folded his arms and looked down at his toes. ''You sure know how to bolster a guy's ego,'' he said softly.

She was immediately contrite. ''All I'm asking for is a chance to breathe. I had no idea you'd even consider marriage.''

''Why not?''

''Because—because I'm not the sort of sophisticated, liberal-minded woman you'd want to be married to.''

''You have your own brand of sophistication,'' Spencer argued sensibly. ''And liberal-minded feminists are a dime a dozen. They've lost their appeal for me.''

''But I'm so old-fashioned. We look at things so differently.''

''I'm beginning to appreciate old-fashioned.''

"I'm traditional. I like being the lady of the house and cooking blueberry muffins. I don't even believe in sex before marriage! At least, not exactly."

"If we get married that won't be a problem."

"You're being glib. This is serious. And besides, there's one other thing, an important thing. You haven't even mentioned love."

He hadn't. Good Lord, how could he ask her to marry him when he hadn't even told her he loved her? Then again, how could she doubt that he did? After all, he'd just sunk his life savings into half of her hotel when he had no earthly use for it. But he hadn't said he loved her, not in so many words. He should have realized how important that was.

He stood up suddenly, feeling agitated, wanting to *do* something to fix this fiasco but not having the vaguest notion of what that something might be. Then a crazy idea popped into his head and began to jell with almost no effort on his part. There was only one way to sweep Bonnie off her feet; he needed a bigger broom.

"Bonnie, please, just forget I said anything about an engagement, all right?"

"All—all right," she answered.

"Can we still have dinner together?"

She hesitated. "No, I can't. My finances are a bit tight right now."

"I wasn't suggesting we go dutch." He felt almost insulted. *Insulted*, that a woman wanted to pay her own way? Had his brain turned to oatmeal? "It's my invitation, my treat," he added.

Bonnie suppressed the near-hysterical laugh that threatened at the back of her throat. She'd just turned down a marriage proposal, and he wanted to take her out on a date? "All right," she agreed. "If we serve dinner early to our own guests, I can be ready by about nine."

"Perfect." He stood decisively. "I hope you don't mind if I disappear again for a couple of hours. I have a few errands to run."

Bonnie wandered around in a daze for what was left of the afternoon, mechanically completing the cleaning chores she'd started earlier. If she could just keep herself busy, she thought, she wouldn't have to think about all the ramifications of this crazy afternoon.

But no matter how she occupied herself, the questions fluttered around inside her head like giant, extremely energetic butterflies.

First she allowed only the less personal matters to filter through to her consciousness. She could sign those papers, and in the blink of an eye she'd be rid of Kenny. But was she trading in one set of problems for another? Just a few days ago she'd wished she could be something besides Spencer's boss. But his partner? What kind of a partner would he be, anyway?

She and Spencer were bound to have disagreements sometimes, just as any business partners would. But he was so strong and determined—ten times stronger than Kenny. How could she hope to stand up for herself against him?

Of course, Spencer would have to be more sensitive and practical than Kenny. Then again, how could she know that for sure? An employer-employee relationship was a far cry from a partnership. Who could tell how Spencer might react to having the responsibility of ownership thrust on him?

Gradually she allowed herself to consider the really troubling question: why hadn't she jumped at Spencer's marriage proposal? She must be crazy! She'd already sworn she wouldn't settle for anything but a long-term relationship with him. Yet when he'd offered her that on a silver platter, she'd said no.

Why?

Not because he was too strong, she decided as she opened the refrigerator, staring into it desultorily. She'd turned him down because he didn't love her.

He did seem bound and determined to take care of her. He'd offered to buy half a hotel toward that end. But that wasn't love. And marrying her just so he could protect her was going a bit too far.

He must have realized that already, she thought, biting her lower lip painfully. At her mention of the word *love* the proposal had died on his lips.

But you love him, her trouble-making inner voice reminded her. What was she going to do about that? If and when he became her partner, she'd be seeing him day in and day out. How could she handle that? Even Kenny's unwanted takeover might be preferable to a constant reminder that the man she loved was a completely inappropriate match who didn't love her back.

Deciding to embark on a task that matched her black mood, Bonnie started to clean out the refrigerator. Thankfully the sound of the bell at the front desk diverted her attention. Since she was more than likely the only one available to answer the bell, she hastily wiped her hands, removed her apron and headed for the lobby.

But it wasn't a guest who waited for her at the front desk. A delivery man greeted her with an arm load of yellow roses.

Chapter Ten

Bonnie signed for the flowers, fumbled for a tip from the change she kept behind the desk, then opened the card with shaking hands. Why was she trembling? They were just flowers. Beautiful, romantic flowers.

"For no special reason except that you ought to have some flowers," the card read. It was signed, "Your reluctant knight in shining armor." Well, there was no doubting whom that described. "Reluctant" was the operative word. Sending flowers couldn't possibly come naturally to him. He'd probably had to force himself.

Yet he did send them. The gesture had to mean something.

The scent of roses caused a thrill of pure feminine delight to course through her. Her head was spinning as she wandered upstairs, clutching the flowers, the refrigerator completely forgotten.

Preparing dinner that evening for the hotel's guests was a strange affair. Apparently Kenny had ceased to care about menus; at least, nothing was written on the chalkboard as of five o'clock. Bonnie made an executive decision, since there was no one else about to consult with: chicken-fried steak, mashed potatoes with gravy, sugar snap peas, corn bread and apple pie. She chose a menu she could prepare in her sleep, since she didn't dare put any trust in her ability to concentrate.

Spencer didn't even show up until dinner was well underway.

"Sorry to be so late," he apologized quickly as he donned an apron and jumped into the preparations. He took over the corn bread as Bonnie returned her attention to the sizzling steak.

She watched him, though, out of the corner of her eye. He handled the cast-iron skillet like an expert now. She'd really hate losing him as a maid, but somehow she doubted that he'd continue wearing an apron once he was an official hotel owner.

Who *would* do the housework? she wondered.

"Thank you for the flowers," she said after a few moments of awkward silence.

He gave her a lopsided, almost self-conscious grin. "Did you really like them? I wasn't sure of the color. The red ones and the pink ones looked pretty, too."

"I like yellow," she said. So, he'd actually gone to the florists and picked out the flowers? That was a nice touch.

They exchanged few words during the rest of the dinner preparations. Bonnie was concentrating on getting everything on the table as quickly as possible so she'd have time to get ready for her "date." Despite herself, she was looking forward to the evening with more excitement than was called for. Flowers had a way of distorting her sense of reality.

She slipped away as soon as was practical, resisting the urge to run up the stairs. She had exactly an hour to get ready, and she didn't even know what she wanted to wear.

As soon as she had gained the privacy of her room, she flung open the closet, examined the skimpy contents, then moaned in despair. The only appropriate dress she had was the topaz silk, and it reminded her too much of that awful night she'd discovered Spencer's deceit. Besides, she wanted to wear something new, something Spencer hadn't seen.

Everything she owned was so casual! Except...she dug to the very back of her closet, at last laying her hands on the garment bag she sought. She pulled it out, hung it on the closet door and unzipped it. Yes!

It was a ruffly blue taffeta gown she'd bought for her senior prom. She'd saved her baby-sitting money for months, fully expecting Kenny Chapman to break down and ask her to the dance. A ridiculous expectation on her part, she mused with a wry smile, given that Kenny had never shown a shred of anything but brotherly interest in her. She'd never worn the dress.

Quickly she donned a slip and stepped into the gown, then appraised herself in her full-length mirror. She adored the ruffles and the way the crisp taffeta rustled when she walked. But the design of the dress was a bit young for her now, she decided. Thank goodness she'd learned to sew, on top of all her other domestic talents.

In less than thirty minutes she'd given the high-necked dress an off-the-shoulder effect. After removing a couple of the fussy bows and changing the way the sash fastened, she deemed it an acceptably adult dress. Though it still wasn't terribly sophisticated, it suited her to a tee.

At a couple of minutes before nine, she was just getting ready to head downstairs to the lobby, where she assumed Spencer would meet her, when someone tapped lightly on her door. Her heart seemed to slam against the wall of her chest before taking up an erratic rhythm.

Why such a reaction? she thought as she took a deep breath before opening the door. But she knew the answer to that when she saw him standing there—in a tuxedo, of all things! He was the most devastatingly masculine, sexy thing she'd ever laid eyes on.

Spencer had to swallow twice before any words could pass through his constricted throat. And even then, the words he spoke weren't the flowery, romantic compliments he'd rehearsed. Somehow those just didn't seem sufficient to describe the awe-inspiring sight of Bonnie in blue taffeta ruffles.

"I've never seen you look more beautiful," he said, his words barely above a whisper. Maybe it wasn't the most original line in the world, he thought, but what it lacked in originality it made up for in sincerity. Tonight Bonnie wasn't just attractive and sexy; she was wreathed in magic.

"Um, thanks," she replied with an uncharacteristic shyness, her eyes downcast. But then she looked up and smiled, and her gaze seemed to caress him. Or was that only his imagination? "You look pretty good yourself," she added.

What came next? he thought as he tried to regain his dangerously skewed equilibrium. Earlier he'd failed miserably when trying to sweep Bonnie off her feet. He was determined to correct the problem this evening, but he was having a hard time not letting *her* sweep *him* away.

At last some appropriately poetic words came to mind. "If you're ready, our chariot awaits us," he said, taking her hand and slowly bringing it to his lips, his eyes never leaving hers.

She grinned, obviously appreciating his effort at gallantry. "Next you'll be telling me we're off to the ball in a silver pumpkin drawn by four white mice."

"You're not too far off," he murmured, thinking of the transportation that actually did await.

They descended the stairs at a regal pace. Bonnie looked at him questioningly as he opened the front door with a flourish and ushered her through. But then her attention wavered, and her eyes became riveted on the silver stretch limousine that crouched in the driveway.

"Spencer, you didn't!"

"I did. I wanted nothing but the best for tonight."

"Since this is a business dinner, can you write this off on your income tax?" she quipped as the uniformed chauffeur opened the back door. Just the same, Spencer could tell she was impressed. So far, so good.

"Depends on how much business we get done."

He solicitously made sure she was tucked safely inside before sliding in across from her. He watched with undisguised pleasure as Bonnie checked out everything in the limo, from the plush velvet upholstery to the mobile telephone to the chilling champagne. The smile remained on her lips, but her eyes grew cautious.

"Spencer, what's this all about?"

"This is not for you to question, but to enjoy," he responded, having anticipated that very reaction from her.

She shrugged and leaned back against the soft blue velvet with a sigh. "I haven't drunk champagne in years," she said with a dreamy look in her eyes.

"Well, let's remedy that." He opened the bottle of imported bubbles with practiced efficiency, then filled two crystal flutes. "Uh-uh, don't drink yet," he said when he saw Bonnie's lips approaching the rim of her glass. "We have to do this right."

"Oh?"

"A toast. To..." He paused, searching for something innocuous to celebrate. "To the continued prosperity of the Sweetwater Inn."

Nodding, she touched her glass to his, but Spencer didn't miss the shadow of doubt that passed briefly across her face. What was troubling her, he wondered?

"Wait a minute, one more thing," he said, again stopping her from taking a sip of champagne. He brought his hand behind hers so that their arms were entwined. "Now we can drink."

The gesture had brought them close—too close, Spencer thought as he took a long sip of the golden liquid. Her light scent teased him, her tumble of golden curls begged for his touch, and her fathomless gray-green eyes held him spellbound. He leaned a fraction of an inch closer and so did she. Their lips brushed lightly. Spencer's body came alive.

"The chauffeur," Bonnie whispered against his mouth, casting a worried glance toward their driver.

"He's trained not to notice," Spencer murmured, lightly nipping her lower lip with his teeth. But after one final, lingering kiss he made himself pull away. Seduction in the back seat of a limo would be out of sync with the romantic tone of the evening, and he wouldn't allow himself to sway from the agenda he had in mind.

It was funny, but he was enjoying this old-fashioned romance stuff a lot more than he'd anticipated. He'd set a goal of creating a perfect fantasy evening for Bonnie, at first believing that he'd have to force himself into the role of chivalrous suitor. But every step of the art of courtly love turned out to be an exciting challenge, from selecting just the right flowers to saying just the right thing. And most of it came naturally for him, as if suddenly he realized he'd been born in the wrong century.

This wouldn't be happening so easily with any other woman, he decided. Perhaps that was because no woman's happiness had ever meant so much to him. Pleasing her was suddenly all that mattered. He didn't mind putting Bonnie on a pedestal, because he felt she'd earned that place in his life.

His colleagues would pass out from shock if they could see him now. He chuckled.

"What's so funny?" Bonnie asked, sounding genuinely curious.

"I was just thinking how things have changed since that day I answered your Help Wanted ad. I walked into the inn, so superior, thinking I had all the answers and that I was going to enlighten the Southern belle, shatter all her preconceived notions about gender roles and stereotypes."

"You did. I was prejudiced toward you because you were a man. I didn't think you could possibly be a good housekeeper. You showed me a thing or two."

"No, you showed me," he said softly.

"Showed you what?"

"That not every woman has to have a fast-track career in order to have a satisfying, fulfilled existence. That there's nothing wrong with cleaning and cooking and taking care of people as a way of life. And that a woman with traditional values isn't necessarily ignorant or uninformed about her choices."

"You learned all that from me?"

"Uh-huh." But he hadn't intended on getting so serious so early in the evening.

"You taught me how to stand up for myself," said Bonnie.

Spencer shook his head. "You would have figured that out on your own. You're strong in ways I never dreamed."

Not that strong, Bonnie thought, gazing out the smoked-glass window at the waxing moon just peeking above the mountaintops. She wasn't strong enough to resist the mood Spencer was so skillfully weaving around her. He'd figured out how to punch every one of her buttons. No matter how strong and capable she might be, a part of her still longed to be pampered, petted and protected like a china doll—at least occasionally. That was exactly what Spencer was doing with this carefully orchestrated evening.

Again she had to wonder why. She'd already asked once, but now she'd keep her questions to herself. She wouldn't risk ruining one of the most enjoyable nights of her life.

"Enjoyable" was a gross understatement, she decided halfway through her chateaubriand. The limo had dropped them at the elegant Lakeside Supper Club, and everyone from the doorman to the maître d' to the wine steward had treated her like a princess. She and Spencer

were seated at the best table in the house, somewhat se-
cluded from the rest of the diners, with an excellent view
of the small mirrorlike mountain lake that gave the restaurant its name.

Then there was Spencer's attention. His golden eyes
never seemed to leave her. Every word he said was just
the right one. He flattered her mercilessly, yet without a
trace of insincerity. He touched her frequently, sometimes running a feather-light finger up her bare arm or
smoothing a strand of her hair away from her forehead.

Every touch ran straight to the center of her being,
striking home with uncanny accuracy. She wasn't sure
what he was after with this slow-dance of seduction, but
she knew he was succeeding at something. She wanted
Spencer Guthrie, body and soul. She loved him and she
wanted to be his wife. She wanted to spend the rest of her
life making him happy.

With a secret smile, she let her mind skitter over the
possibilities. The differences between them didn't seem
to matter so much now. But then she remembered the
way he'd backed off at the mention of the word *love*, and
doubts crowded in once again. That was one difference
of opinion she couldn't compromise on. Love had to be
part of the bargain.

When they were lingering over their bananas flambé,
the small orchestra struck up a sentimental old song from
the forties.

"Care to dance?" Spencer inquired politely.

She couldn't think of anything she'd enjoy more than
an excuse to linger in his arms. She nodded her assent,
and in a few moments they were holding each other close,
swaying to the big-band music.

It was almost time for the evening's climax, Spencer thought, letting his hand skim over the creamy flesh of her bare shoulders. He'd laid the groundwork as carefully as possible. He'd have to leave the rest up to fate.

"It's warm in here," he murmured in her ear, twirling her gently toward the edge of the dance floor. "Why don't we step outside onto the terrace?"

"Mmm, good idea," she responded in the dreamy voice she'd used all evening. He considered that an encouraging sign.

They stepped through French doors onto a deserted flagstone terrace that was almost smothered in wisteria. Outside it was no cooler than inside the air-conditioned restaurant, Spencer reckoned, but a slight breeze made it seem less stale. Hand in hand, they ambled over to a low wall bordering the shadowy terrace and gazed out at the glass-smooth lake bathed in moonlight.

The sound of the band was muffled to low, tinny background music. The only other sound to greet them was the rustle of the breeze in the wisteria climbing on the trellis overhead, and an occasional cricket chirp.

"Um, Bonnie," he began, searching his memory for the poetic speech he'd agonized over earlier. He'd even gone so far as to write down the words and rehearse them in the shower just a couple of hours ago. Where were those beautiful words now?

"Yes? Did you want to say something?"

"Not exactly." He squeezed his eyes closed, racking his brain to recall his wonderful speech. It remained, perversely, just out of reach of his consciousness.

Bonnie sighed expansively. "This certainly is a beautiful night. Such a nice breeze, all full of the scent of summer. And have you ever seen a prettier moon?"

Moon! That triggered part of his paralyzed memory. "The moon isn't one-half as beautiful as you, with your lovely face bathed in moonbeams."

"Hmm? Oh, I'm sorry, I wasn't listening. I saw a fish jump on the lake. Do you suppose there's good bass fishing down there?"

Thank God, she hadn't heard him. He'd sounded totally inane. And here he'd been so proud of himself, wearing the mantle of chivalry so adeptly. Now it was catching up with him. He was falling apart at the critical moment.

Just spit it out, Guthrie, he ordered himself. "Bonnie?" He had to make sure she was with him one hundred percent this time.

"Yes?"

"I have something I want to give you." He reached into his breast pocket. His fingers closed around...empty space. Frantically he searched all of his pockets. Then he remembered. He'd set the little box on his dresser, where he wouldn't forget it. And he'd forgotten it.

That part doesn't matter, he tried to tell himself. *Get to the good stuff.*

"Spencer, is something wrong?"

"No. I mean yes. I wanted to do this just right, and now I'm flubbing it all up, but I've got to do it anyway." He looked straight at her then and took both of her hands into his. "Bonnie, you're the sweetest, loveliest woman I've ever known and I love you. I love you so much it hurts. And I intend to go on loving you even if we don't always agree on everything. What I'm saying, or trying to say, that is—"

Awkwardly he dropped to one knee. "Bonnie Chapman, will you marry me? I bought a ring and everything, except I left it at home. It's a nice ring, I think you'll like it. I picked out a traditional setting, in white gold, 'cause I didn't think you'd like one of those modern geometric things. But we can exchange the one I got if you don't like it—"

"Spencer, will you stop babbling? I can't squeeze a yes in edgewise."

He did stop. He didn't think he could talk if his life depended on it. He also couldn't stand. He had a killer cramp in his right thigh, but he didn't care. He saw everything he ever wanted or needed in Bonnie's shining eyes.

When he made no move to stand, she knelt down until they were nose to nose. "Yes," she said succinctly, "I'll marry you. Just name the time and place."

Relief swept over him. "The wedding might have to take place right here, if I don't get this cramp out of my leg."

"Oh, here, let me help you. I didn't realize . . ." She hauled him to his feet, then walked him around the terrace until the cramp subsided.

"Sorry about that," Spencer finally said as he sank onto a wrought-iron bench, rubbing his thigh. "I didn't intend for the evening to go quite like this."

Bonnie affectionately ruffled his hair. "Poor Spencer. You've really done yourself in with all this romantic nonsense, haven't you?"

"It's not nonsense!" he argued. "Besides, you make it sound like I struggled. I didn't. Once I got started it came quite naturally to me—the flowers, the champagne, the candlelight. It was the stress of the marriage proposal that finally got me."

"Was it that bad?"

"Only until you said yes."

"Oh, Spencer, I do love you. I don't mind telling you now that I've been kind of worried about how things would turn out, but as long as you love me I'm sure we'll be able to work out the problems." She leaned forward to kiss him.

He pulled back, denying her access to his lips. "Problems? What problems?"

"Well…" She chewed her lower lip. "I just have a few questions. Like who'll be in charge?"

Spencer attempted to mask his horrified reaction. "Bonnie, I know you're somewhat old-fashioned, but you don't actually believe someone has to wear the pants in a marriage, do you? Because I intend for our marriage to be an equal partnership. And if you don't see it that way…" He halted.

Bonnie was laughing. "I wasn't talking about our marriage, silly. I was talking about the inn."

For the second time that evening, Spencer was overcome with relief. "Thank heavens. You had me worried there for a minute. Now what about the inn?"

"If I agree to the purchase—and I plan to—each of us will own fifty percent, so who's in charge?" she asked. "And who gets to be the maid?"

Now it all made sense to Spencer—her reticence this afternoon, the occasional pensiveness this evening and the downright worried look on her face now. After what she'd been through these past few weeks, could he blame her? She was trading in one overbearing business partner for another, albeit more sensitive one.

He was quick to reassure her. "I'm an innkeeper in name only," he said. "The Sweetwater is yours to run as you see fit. All I ask is that you let me live there. And as for the housekeeping, quite frankly soon I won't have time to do it. I'm taking on a full teaching load in the fall. But I'd advise you to seriously consider hiring another housekeeper. Keeping that place running is a big job.''

"Too big for a little girl like me?" He could almost feel her bristles popping up. She learned fast.

"I'd just like you to save some leisure time for me, that's all. I'm pretty demanding."

Bonnie giggled. "That's a funny thing for you to say. You aren't going all macho on me, are you? I was just getting used to the concept of a liberated man."

"I intend to be every bit as liberated as you."

"Now *that* sounds like a challenge." She raised one eyebrow in mock bravado as she clasped her hands behind his neck. "Just watch me give *you* a lesson in assertiveness."

Epilogue

"Come in!" Spencer called out at the soft tapping on his office door.

Randy Hoskins opened the door just wide enough that he could slip his tall lean frame inside. "Have a minute, Professor?"

"Sure. Have a seat."

"About my grade," Randy began, sliding into the wooden chair across from Spencer's desk, "why an Incomplete? Why didn't you just fail me?"

"Randy, you knew when you signed up for my class that no one gets out without doing the employment assignment—not even me, it turns out. But you don't deserve to fail, either. You've met every other objective of the course and you aced the final."

Randy gave a long-suffering sigh. "All right, I guess there's no way out of it. Is the housekeeping job at the Sweetwater Inn still open?"

"Yup. Now stop looking like I've given you a death sentence. You might be surprised at what you'll get out of the experience. Look what happened to Jenny. She discovered a whole new career as a fire fighter."

"That's different. There's no way I'll find my true calling as a housekeeper."

"Well, there *are* other fringe benefits. For example, in my case—" He was about to explain about all the new insight he'd gained, but he was interrupted by another knock on his door. "Come in," he called again.

His heart gave an extra thump when he saw Bonnie tentatively poking her head around the edge of the door. Just the sight of her still had the ability to move him. He suspected it always would. Her hair was in its usual disarray, and her cheeks were flushed a becoming pink. "It's not a bad time, is it?" she asked, almost breathlessly.

"No. Actually, sweetheart, your timing couldn't be better." He stood and drew Bonnie into the small room. She was holding a red plastic garment bag, which he took from her and hung on the door. Then he planted a kiss on her lips, designed to curl her toes.

Randy stared at them, wide-eyed. "You're Ms. Chapman, aren't you?"

"*Mrs.* Chapman," Bonnie corrected him gently.

"Soon to be Mrs. Guthrie," Spencer added, smiling indulgently. "Bonnie, this is the student I was telling you about, Randy Hoskins."

"Oh, the one who wants to apply for the maid's job?" Bonnie took his hand and shook it. "It's nice to meet you. Just give me a call some time next week and we can talk about it."

Randy managed a stiff nod, but his eyes stayed glued on Spencer, as if he couldn't believe what he saw. "You two are getting married?"

"Uh-huh," Bonnie and Spencer answered together. "Tomorrow's the big day. Look," Spencer added, unzipping the garment bag. "Here's my tux." His smile widened as he revealed the crisp black jacket with its satin-striped lapels and accompanying pleated white shirt.

"I was passing right by the cleaners," Bonnie explained in an aside to Spencer, "so I picked it up for you. Now, I really have to get back to the inn. I put Kenny to work doing laundry this morning and things have been out of kilter ever since."

Spencer couldn't help laughing out loud as he pictured Kenny trying to master the ancient washing machine. As good as Kenny was at delegating chores, he was awful at executing them himself. But Spencer had to give him credit for at least trying to help out.

Bonnie joined in with a giggle or two of her own. "He's still surly and superior on occasion, but he's come a long way the last couple of weeks. I think being free of any real responsibilities agrees with him. Just the same, I'll be relieved to see him off at the airport next week."

She returned the kiss Spencer had given her a few moments earlier, and he discovered his own toes were curling; then she was gone.

When he returned his somewhat flustered attention to Randy, he was met with a look of such blatant skepticism he almost started laughing again. "I told you there were fringe benefits," he said.

"Sounds like some sort of reverse sexual harassment to me," Randy accused, only half joking. "I mean, after all, she is your boss."

"Technically she's now my partner, but we won't get into that," Spencer retorted, a bit more sharply than he intended. "The important point is that I'm marrying her, not harassing her."

"But when you first took that job, you told the class you were going to teach the Southern belle a lesson in equality. What happened?"

"I learned a few lessons of my own, that's what happened." He leaned back in his chair and closed his eyes for a moment, his irritation vanishing as quickly as it had come. "And everyone should have such a teacher," he added softly.

*   *   *   *   *

COMING NEXT MONTH

#712 HARVEY'S MISSING—Peggy Webb
A Diamond Jubilee Title!
Janet Hall was in search of her missing weekend dog, Harvey, but
what she found was Dan Albany, who claimed Harvey was *his*
week*day* dog. Would the two ever agree on anything?

#713 JUST YOU AND ME—Rena McKay
The Loch Ness monster was less elusive than the blue-eyed
MacNorris men of Norbrae Castle. Vacationing Lynn Marquet
was falling fast for Mike MacNorris, one of the mystifying
Scottish clansmen . . . or was she?

#714 MONTANA HEAT—Dorsey Kelley
Nanny Tracy Wilborough expected to find peace of mind in
Montana. What she hadn't counted on was exciting rodeo
performer Nick Roberts lassoing her heart!

#715 A WOMAN'S TOUCH—Brenda Trent
When Troy Mayhan first met neighbor Shelly Hall, they literally
fell into each other's arms. Now the sexy ex-football player was
determined to have her fall again—in love with him!

#716 JUST NEIGHBORS—Marcine Smith
Loner Wyatt Neville had never had a sweet tooth—or been
tempted to indulge in romance—until delectable Angela Cowan
moved her cookie factory next door to his home. . . .

#717 HIS BRIDE TO BE—Lisa Jackson
The contract said she was his bride to be for two weeks only. But
two weeks was all it took for Hale Donovan to know that Valerie
Pryce was his love for a lifetime.

AVAILABLE THIS MONTH:

#706 NEVER ON SUNDAE
Rita Rainville

#707 DOMESTIC BLISS
Karen Leabo

#708 THE MARK OF ZORRO
Samantha Grey

**#709 A CHILD CALLED
MATTHEW**
Sara Grant

#710 TIGER BY THE TAIL
Pat Tracy

#711 SEALED WITH A KISS
Joan Smith

proudly presents

Taming Natasha
by
NORA ROBERTS

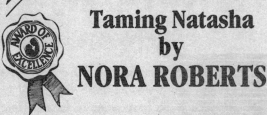

Once again, award-winning author Nora Roberts weaves her
special brand of magic this month in TAMING NATASHA
(SSE #583). Toy shop owner Natasha Stanislaski is a pussycat
with Spence Kimball's little girl, but to Spence himself she's as
ornery as a caged tiger. Will some cautious loving sheath her
claws and free her heart from captivity?

TAMING NATASHA, by Nora Roberts, has been selected to receive
a special laurel—the Award of Excellence. This month look for
the distinctive emblem on the cover. It lets you know there's
something truly special inside.

Available now

M

AVAILABLE NOW—

the books you've been waiting for by one of
America's top romance authors!

DIANA PALMER

DUETS

Ten years ago Diana Palmer published her very first
romances. Powerful and dramatic, these gripping tales
of love are everything you have come to expect from
Diana Palmer.

This month some of these titles are available again in
DIANA PALMER DUETS—a special three-book collection. Each book has two wonderful stories plus an introduction by the author. You won't want to miss them!

Book 1
**SWEET ENEMY
LOVE ON TRIAL**

Book 2
**STORM OVER THE LAKE
TO LOVE AND CHERISH**

Book 3
**IF WINTER COMES
NOW AND FOREVER**

Available now at your favorite retail outlet.

 *Silhouette Books*®